THE TINHORN MURDER CASE

Doc Beaumont was certainly not a treacherous back-shooter, but he was arrogant and rash enough to believe he could conduct his own defence and bedazzle the judge and jury. Fortunately for the gambling dude, Larry and Stretch set out to prove his innocence in a more old-fashioned way. While Doc rehearsed spellbinding speeches in the County Jail, the doughty drifters dug into the crises confronting the local lawmen — with spectacularly violent results.

MARSHALL GROVER

THE TINHORN MURDER CASE

A Larry & Stretch Western

Complete and Unabridged

LINFORD
Leicester

First published in Australia in 1984 by
Horwitz Grahame Books Pty Limited
Australia

First Linford Edition
published November 1994
by arrangement with
Horwitz Grahame Books Pty Limited
Australia

British Library CIP Data

Grover, Marshall
    Larry & Stretch: the tinhorn murder case.
    —Large print ed.—
    Linford western library
    I. Title II. Series
    823 [F]

    ISBN 0–7089–7599–2

Published by
F. A. Thorpe (Publishing) Ltd.
Anstey, Leicestershire

Set by Words & Graphics Ltd.
Anstey, Leicestershire
Printed and bound in Great Britain by
T. J. Press (Padstow) Ltd., Padstow, Cornwall

This book is printed on acid-free paper

1

Treachery's Victim

MARVIN QUEEL, the schoolteacher of Purdyville, Iowa, had been a troubled man these past four weeks.

"And you aren't the only one," reflected the town's only lawman. Marshal Olaf Eriksen was filling the rocking chair on the porch of his office, watching the schoolteacher advance in his direction. "One of many you are, mister. One of the many good citizens with their life savings in the Toliver Bank. I know what you're gonna ask — and it's just no use."

A shade under six feet tall, Marvin Queel was soberly garbed, a studious, sensitive-featured man whose tendency to stoop seemed to have increased since the disaster of four weeks ago. Until then, crime and violence, any kind of upheaval, had never been heard of in this small farming community; Purdyville, Iowa, had little in common with the burgeoning towns of the frontiers to the west. The looting of the Toliver Bank, an independent enterprise carrying no insurance, had reduced its clients to near-bankruptcy. Cunningly planned and executed, the hold-up had caught banker Toliver and his cashier with their guard down and the safe open; it had taken less than seven minutes for the masked desperadoes to empty the safe and make good their escape.

"Dare I enquire . . . ?" The school-teacher began on reaching the porch.

"Same answer, Mister Queel," said Eriksen. "You know how sorry I am, but it's been a whole month and the only news I get is bad. No trace of the bank-robbers. Slim chance the bank's funds'll ever be recovered."

"It is indeed a tragedy," sighed Marvin. "For everybody, of course. I must think of the other clients at this unhappy time."

"You always were a charitable gent," Eriksen complimented him.

"I'm sure, Marshal Eriksen, you've done everything possible," said Marvin.

"Had a good posse backing me when I chased the raiders north," muttered Eriksen. "We stayed after 'em two and a half days as you'll recall. Mister Dolan at the telegraph office wired every peace officer within a hundred miles and, with his own money — what was left of it — Darien Toliver called in the Pinkertons. Everything possible has been done, that's a fact."

"I must be realistic and accept it," Marvin said dolefully. "They were just — too clever."

"I got my hunch, for what it's worth," offered Eriksen. "Seems to me they must've shared their loot and separated first time they spelled their horses. Then they took off in all directions, each man killing his back-trail."

"Despite the good efforts of all parties

involved, the hunt was doomed from the start," Marvin supposed.

"I'm sorry for every citizen who's a loser, but maybe sorriest for you," declared Eriksen.

"You shouldn't be," shrugged Marvin. "The losses of other folk are greater than ours."

"Maybe so," frowned Eriksen. "But when I think of your wife, fine lady that she is, and those beautiful daughters of yours — all four of 'em . . . "

"We'll manage," said Marvin, turning away. "Somehow."

His wife used that word at supper-time in the somewhat apprehensive atmosphere of the dining room in their rented home. Flora Queel, one of Purdyville's most popular matrons, was aging gracefully, retaining her figure and complexion, showing few age-lines; friends and neighbors were wont to remark she was as beautiful as any of her daughters.

"Somehow, Marvin dear, we'll survive this reversal," she said encouragingly.

"This shattering reversal?" he challenged. "Flora, we really *are* in dire straits. The town council rejected my plea for a rise in salary and, on my earnings, we've barely enough for . . ."

"We can help, Papa," offered the youngest daughter, seventeen-year-old Angeline. "We could all get jobs, right Prue?"

"I don't see why not," agreed Prudence, the second eldest.

"Thank you, girls," said their mother. "But you know that's quite impractical, certainly in Purdyville. No opportunities for young ladies of refinement here. I am grateful that your father has educated you to such high standards."

"Be reasonable," Marvin appealed to the quartet of dark-haired, blue-eyed beauties, every one a replica of their attractive mother. "What could you do? Hire yourselves out as farm-girls, wait on table in cafes? I wouldn't hear of it."

"Maybe *I* have the answer," frowned

5

Ruth, the nineteen-year-old.

"Ruth, how *could* you?" chided Josephine, the eldest daughter. "Besides, neither Mother nor Papa would ever permit it."

"Mister de Groot's the richest man in Purdyville . . . " began Ruth.

"A widower these past ten years, and with a roving eye," Flora said disdainfully. "Moreover, he's older than your dear father. It's unthinkable, Ruth."

"A lot of men marry much younger women," argued Ruth.

"A barbaric practice," protested Marvin.

"Well, I'm willing," shrugged Ruth. "I mean, it's the family that counts. I'm sure Mister de Groot would take care of us all and — and I'm ready to make the sacrifice."

"Very noble," sniffed Josephine. "But absolutely out of the question. There has to be another way. Papa, what of your brother who went west to make his fortune? Do you mind so much?"

"Mind what?" asked Marvin.

"Well, you know what Jo means," giggled Angeline. "You always speak of him with affection, but you're the one called him the black sheep of your family. Your very words, Papa."

"Bernard was a wayward boy and even wilder when he came of age and ran away," Marvin said with a wistful grin. "We had nothing in common, but I couldn't help liking him. He was a whimsical fellow." He sighed and shook his head. "No, Josphine, I couldn't beg a loan from your Uncle Bernard. I still have my pride."

"It will be difficult for us, but we'll manage," declared Flora. "Sometimes I think we're over-eating. So, if we tighten our belts as the saying goes . . . "

The sisters traded covert glances. Their father was a lean man, their mother as trim-waisted as any of them, and without benefit of whalebone corsetting. For the refined Queels of Purdyville, the future had never looked blacker.

★ ★ ★

This same evening, fickle Fate was conspiring against a stranger in the bustling mining and ranching township of Cluff City, Colorado. For Vincent Beaumont, M.D., the future would very soon become uncertain, to say the least. A handsome dandy of mixed parentage — Doc's mother had been a feisty Irishwoman, his father a cultured scion of New Orleans high society — this haughty veteran of the green-covered gaming tables had his pet aversions. One of these was his true profession. He was a qualified physician and surgeon of impressive talent, but preferred to keep this to himself. True, his medical gear traveled with him wherever he roamed, but always secreted in his packroll. Give Doc his choice, he'd settle for poker every time. Poker was his passion, far more fascinating to him than the treating of wounds, the setting of broken limbs, the blubbering of brats laid up with croup, measles or other juvenile ailments.

To the other sporting gentry involved in the game that began within an hour of his arrival he had given his real name, describing himself as an itinerant gambler. His qualifications as a medical man would be, as usual, his own well-kept secret. Now, with the game nearing its end, he was encountering another of his pet aversions. Doc despised sore losers. And the man called Beau Mosser was certainly that, though he too wore the rig of the professional sporting man.

"Cool that mean temper of yours, Mosser," chided Erwin Fogel, owner of the Siren Saloon and organizer of this poker party. The other players, local businessmen, were equally as disapproving of the sore loser's attitude; though somewhat taciturn, the stranger had conducted himself as a gentleman and was undoubtedly the most skilled player present — as evidenced by his piled winnings. "Beaumont's no sharper. You got no right to . . . "

"He wins too regular for my liking," scowled Mosser, his spite-filled eyes on Doc's handsome visage. Handsome it was, Doc being fastidious about his looks. The mustache was well-clipped, the features downright aristocratic, the clothes custom-made; Doc Beaumont and sartorial elegance were old cronies. "I'm calling him a lousy cheat and I'm not taking it back!"

"I'm a loser too, Mosser," said Gus Blackstone, the dry-good merchant. "And I'm telling you Mister Beaumont's some helluva poker-player and *that's* why he's a regular winner."

"Thank you, Mister Blackstone," drawled Doc. "I salute you, mine host and these other gentlemen as worthy opponents." Cold-eyeing Mosser, he added, "But not you, sir."

"The hell with you and your smart talk, you sharping dude!" snarled Mosser.

With that, he lost control of himself completely, half-rose, leaned across the table and, before anybody could

10

intervene, gave the stranger the back of his hand. Calling Doc a card-sharp had been unwise. To compound the insult in this fashion was an even worse mistake, as he was soon to learn. Doc was out of his chair so quickly that Fogel and the other men blinked in astonishment. Just as quickly, Mosser was separated from his seat by Doc, helpless in his grasp. By collar of coat and slack of pants, Doc frogmarched him across the barroom to the entrance and hurled him into the street. He then flicked an imaginary speck of dust from the velvet-edged lapel of his frock-coat and unhurriedly returned to the poker table, there to be commended by the other losers.

As he stowed his winnings in his wallet, he smiled urbanely at Fogel.

"A pleasant battle of wits — marred only by the ungentlemanly conduct of a sore loser," he remarked. "If you'll name your pleasure, my friends, the last round is on me."

"No, on me," insisted Fogel. "Herb . . . "

He made to signal a bartender, but then Mosser was trudging in again, disheveled, begrimed and wild-eyed, and pointing at Doc.

"I demand satisfaction!" he raged. "You hear me, sharper? I'll be waiting for you out front!"

He cursed obscenely, turned on his heel and departed. Fogel grimaced irritably, caught the bartender's eye, then assured Doc,

"You don't have to mess with that dumb hothead."

"Of course not," Doc serenely agreed. "He's hardly worth the trouble and, besides, I'm opposed to street-fighting. Fools like Mosser never spare a thought for the obvious danger to neutral bystanders."

"Town's too wild already," grouched Blackstone. "You know how many times I've had to replace my street-window this year, Erwin? Three times already." To Doc, he remarked, "Our sheriff and his deputies try hard to keep the rowdies controled, but it's a losing battle. Jerry Dorgan only has but two deputies."

"Miners and cowhands in and out of town all the time," another player complained. "That's the hell of it. There's more rowdyism in the county seat than three lawmen can put down."

"When you're ready to leave, Beaumont, it'd be better if you use the rear exit," urged Fogel.

"Exactly what I had in mind," Doc assured him.

He relaxed while partaking of Fogel's hospitality, maintaining a genial exterior. Not that Fogel's Siren Saloon was his idea of a high-class venue. He could recall with pleasure the most luxuriously appointed casinos of Denver, Cheyenne, Carson City, Santa Fe and other frontier cities, all of which he infinitely preferred. Because Fogel was his host, he concealed his distaste for the bawdy daub from which the saloon took its name. Fogel sat with his back to it, a framed nude of extravagant dimensions coyly crooking a finger. Some siren. A dozen of her kind couldn't lure Doc Beaumont two inches from a poker table, not even if all he held was a pair of deuces.

Not so relaxed were the two mining identities sharing a table near the bar. Ed Chilson, a hefty, well-dressed man of florid complexion and predatory instincts, spoke quietly but urgently to one of his hired hands, a slack-jawed rogue named Milt Wynant.

"That sonofabitch just played right into our hands, Milt."

"Your money's on the dude stranger, huh?" grinned Wynant.

"We have to be sure," insisted Chilson. He and his partner, owners of the Grand Venture Mine in the Sierra Rojo, had ample reason for craving the speedy demise of the sore loser. "And this is a chance too good to pass up. You could handle it, Milt. Hell, what could be easier?"

"Just what're you gettin' at?" frowned Wynant.

"You leave now," said Chilson. "You stay out of sight, but keep your eyes on Mosser. When he trades shots with the dude, all you have to do is make sure he goes down. Do I have to spell it out for you, damn it? Time it right and nobody'll know the difference. If Dorgan wants to arrest anybody, the dude's the obvious patsy. It's a perfect set-up, the best chance we'll ever get."

"Well, all right, but listen now," muttered Wynant. "I know Mosser has to go and I'm willin' to handle it, but it's gonna cost you. Next time out, I draw double my share."

"Agreed," grinned Chilson. "Now get going."

Wynant drained his glass, got to his feet and ambled out. Fifteen minutes later, ready to call it a day, having checked into a hotel a few moments after his arrival, the gambling medico said his goodnights to Fogel and the other losers. He was invited to stop by again, and assured them he would do so. Fogel nodded to the rear exit and Doc headed in that direction. Then, seconds after he had entered the back alley, Mosser came bounding in again, still fuming, still trouble-hungry. He took one look at the vacant chair, swore luridly and gave vent to his frustration.

"Damn yellow-bellied dude sneaked out the back way!"

"Simmer down, Mosser," advised Fogel. "Beaumont isn't interested in you any more — to put it mildly."

"I got a score to settle with him!" snarled Mosser. "And I aim to settle it with a bullet — damn him to hell!"

He retreated through the batwings, dashed to the side alley and ran to its rear end, drawing a .38 from his armpit holster. In the back alley, sighting the well-tailored stranger strolling south, he aimed too quickly and cut loose.

As the slug sped past his head, Doc

whirled, drew his Colt and returned fire but, by then, Mosser was panic-stricken and dodging frantically. Doc's bullet missed. He grinned contemptuously as Mosser turned to flee and, seeking only to hasten his cowardly challenger on his way, aimed high above Mosser's head and fired again. Something about the report disquieted him; his gunshot's echo seemed overly long — or had another shot merged with his? He saw Mosser throw up his hands, heard his anguished yell and watched him pitch forward to hit the alley's dirt face-first. Throwing a glance over his shoulder, sighting nobody else, he began moving to where Mosser lay. Simultaneously, Fogel, a barkeep and several other men emerged from the saloon's rear doorway, and out of a side alley hustled Cluff City's elder law officer, the tall, bushy-browed Jerry Dorgan, sheriff of Gomez County. Dorgan was brandishing a sawn-off shotgun. Hard on the lawman's heels came a pot-bellied townman whose blunt features

17

were inherited from Teutonic forebears, Dr Emil Schubert, complete with small black valise.

"Everybody make way for the doc," ordered Dorgan, his cold gaze fixed on the stranger. "And you, hand me that iron — butt-first if you know what's good for you."

"Easy, Sheriff," protested Fogel. "Mister Beaumont's a gentleman-gambler. Shooting a man in the back is not his style."

"I got eyes to see with," growled Dorgan.

"I'll surrender my weapon, but only as a gesture of good faith," drawled Doc. He holstered his handsome Colt, unstrapped his ornately-tooled gunbelt, wound it about the holster and passed it to Dorgan. "And now, anticipating your question, I advise you to mount a search for a third party. There had to be more than three shots fired. Mosser was the aggressor. When I heard his shot and felt the wind of his bullet, I turned and retaliated. He was dodging, so I missed him. Then he took to his heels . . . "

"And you let him have it," accused Ed Chilson, moving to the fore.

"Kindly desist," chided Doc. "I'm addressing myself to the sheriff."

"I'll ask the questions, Mister Chilson, if you don't mind," said Dorgan.

"My second bullet was aimed high over his head," Doc told him. "It seemed louder and prolonged, that second report, so obviously a third party triggered the bullet that struck this man."

"I heard three shots," retorted Dorgan. "How about you gents?"

"Three," insisted Chilson.

"Well, it sounded like only three shots," frowned Fogel. "But I'm more inclined to believe Mister Beaumont."

"Let's hear it, Doc," urged Dorgan.

Schubert rose to his feet to announce.

"The bullet entered the back and lodged in the heart. I'll do a post-mortem which will, I'm sure, confirm my preliminary findings. Death would have been instantaneous. Well, no later than a minute after the moment of impact."

"Aimed high, huh?" Dorgan jibed at Doc. "Not high enough, Beaumont. If he was shot from the front, I'd call it self-defense. But a bullet in the back is murder plain and simple, and that's what I'm holdin' you for." He unhitched his manacles. "Hands behind your back."

"By all means." Doc grinned scathingly as he obeyed. "I've no intention of resisting arrest and depriving myself of the pleasure of watching you make a fool of yourself."

"For a back-shooting killer, he's mighty sure of himself," observed Chilson. "In your boots, Sheriff, I wouldn't be taking any lip from the likes of him."

"You are, I presume, the county prosecutor?" enquired Doc.

"No," said Fogel. "He's Ed Chilson, half-owner of the Grand Venture Mine."

"My mistake," smiled Doc. "He blusters in the manner of a typical frontier lawyer of the loud-mouthed type."

"You deserve to hang," scowled Chilson. "Beau Mosser may not have been a likeable feller, but he was a man, and no man should have to die this way — shot in the back by a Fancy Dan tinhorn."

"Couple of you men take the body to the funeral parlor," ordered the sheriff. He hung Doc's belted Colt over a shoulder, rammed the dead man's .38 into his pants-belt and showed his prisoner the business-end of the shotgun. "That's all, dude. Let's go."

In the office fronting the Gomez County Jail, Doc Beaumont made quite an impression on his captors. The younger deputy, fresh-faced Ben Berry, was supposed to be walking the sundown-to-midnight patrol, but had looked in for a quick cup of coffee. The elder deputy, Sam Tragg, was in the habit of dozing on the office couch on such occasions as he drew the midnight to dawn 'graveyard' shift. The cellblock was empty at this time. Lounging in its open doorway was the county jailer, a slender, shaggy-haired Englishman, Theodore Haskin by name, middle-aged, respected by Dorgan and his deputies as being efficient at his chores, if somewhat of a loner short on conversation. Maybe Haskin, more than the others, was most taken aback by the new prisoner's imperious demeanor.

Relieved of the manacles, Doc began emptying his pockets.

"You may search me — that's your prerogative," he remarked to the frowning Dorgan. "But you'll find only my cigars and matches. I presume I'll be allowed smoke. My wallet should be locked in your safe. As it contains better than twenty-five hundred dollars, I'll require a receipt. I'll also require a suitable table."

"Table?" scowled Tragg. He was of an age with the sheriff, nudging forty, and one of the ugliest men Doc had ever seen, a husky, barrel-chested veteran. "Who is this hombre and where does he think he is — a hotel?"

"In for murder," said Dorgan. "Table, Beaumont? What table?"

"For my cell," said Doc. "To be used as a desk. I'll require pen and ink and a supply of writing paper."

"Fixin' to do a heap of writin', huh?" prodded Tragg.

"Notes," Doc said loftily. "For the preparation of my defense."

"Your lawyer'll take care of that," said Dorgan. "We got three lawyers in Cluff City. Hugo Kingfisher is county prosecutor, but that leaves you a choice of the other two."

"Your presumptuousness continues to amaze me," sneered Doc.

"Now look, Beaumont, you got cash aplenty," growled Dorgan, after tallying the prisoner's bankroll. "You can afford . . . "

"As if your first mistake — assuming

me to be a back-shooter — isn't bad enough," chided Doc, "you have the gall to assume I'd entrust my defense to a lame-brained lawyer resident in a brawling, backward hamlet like Cluff City. Preposterous! I will conduct my own defense, confound the attorney for the prosecution, capture the minds of every member of the jury, profoundly impress the judge and prove beyond all reasonable doubt I am innocent of this ridiculous charge!" He turned to Haskin. "And now, if you'll kindly show me to my quarters — you are the turnkey, I take it?"

"Theodore Roland Haskin, at your service, Mister Beaumont," offered the jailer, bowing courteously.

"What the hell's goin' on here?" gasped Tragg. "That's the first time I ever heard Theo talk *that* way to a jailbird!"

"Haskin, you never talk that way to us," complained Dorgan. "Come to think of it, you scarce ever say a word to us."

"Mister Beaumont, this way, if you please," said Haskin. "I think you'll find Cell Five reasonably comfortable."

"One moment," said Doc.

"Certainly," said Haskin.

"You have my permission," Doc informed the grim-visaged Dorgan, "to take whatever cash is necessary from my wallet and ensure the safety of my other personal effects. My room at the Gillette House is to be kept locked for the duration of my incarceration in this miserable bastille. You'll find my horse at the Billings Barn. Kindly see to it that the animal receives the best of care. It's a thoroughbred — naturally." He added, as he turned to follow Haskin into the cellblock. "And don't forget. Pen and ink, paper and a suitable table."

After prisoner and jailer had disappeared into the jailhouse, silence prevailed in Dorgan's office for almost a half-minute. All three lawmen were dumbstruck by the audacity, the arrogance of the dandy who, in due course, would stand trial before Circuit-Judge Elisha Spalding. Tragg flopped to the couch again, shaking his head dazedly. Young Ben Berry gawked at the closed cellblock entrance. Dorgan, first to rally, growled at him.

"Ben boy, you're supposed to be walkin' patrol. What do you think we got here — a peaceful, law-abidin' town? Move your ass!"

"On my way," mumbled Ben, reaching for his shotgun. "Hey, Mister Dorgan, how about this Beaumont feller?"

"He'll have his day in court like any other back-shootin' killer," scowled Dorgan. "Scat!"

Ben departed. Tragg became horizontal again, but not silent.

"I'll ask the same question," he muttered. "How about this Beaumont?"

"Gamblers are a mixed bunch," shrugged Dorgan. "Some of 'em got education. I guess that's why Theo took a shine to him."

"Betcha life," agreed Tragg. "Theo don't talk much, but I got the feelin' he wasn't raised in no hick English town."

"He's a good jailer," said Dorgan. "So, as long as he does his job, he can stay as close-mouthed as he wants."

"Old Etonian," the English jailer was informing Doc, while installing him in Cell 5. "Then Oxford. Sent down, you know, before I could graduate."

"Ne'er-do-well," Doc remarked, but affably.

"Reprobate, spendthrift, disgrace to a noble family, that sort of thing," nodded Haskin, re-securing the door. "You may have known other such expatriates, Mister Beaumont."

"Well, certainly," said Doc. "Frontier folk are a motley lot, to say the least. I've encountered quite a few remittance men and the like. This is, however, my first meeting with an English turnkey."

"Since coming to the New World, I've become an inveterate bookworm," Haskin confided. "I have, as you'll appreciate, little in common with the law officers or, for that matter, with any denizen of this horrendous metropolis, so I'm somewhat of a recluse. I live here in the jail, the only place in Cluff City where I feel safe. I rarely venture forth except of course when Judge Spalding holds court. I do enjoy a good trial . . . "

"You'll enjoy mine," Doc smugly predicted. "I'll bedazzle 'em all, by thunder, you'll see."

"His Honor is a fascinating type, puts on a damn fine show actually," said Haskin. "And old Kingfisher, the county prosecutor, is almost as entertaining. Gruff old toss-pot you know. A trifle backward in the social graces I fear. He gestured toward the rear of the jailhouse. "The end cell on this side. It isn't much, but I call it home. Sheriff Dorgan allows me a little leeway. I've installed shelves for my books and a few creature comforts. Oh, by the way, Mister Beaumont . . . "

"Vincent Beaumont," said Doc. "Just Beaumont will do."

"Theodore Roland Haskin, late of Haskin Abbey, Torquay and Mayfair," nodded Haskin. "Haskin will suffice. A rare pleasure, Beaumont."

"Mutual," smiled Doc, warming to him.

"Decent of you to say so," acknowledged Haskin. "In my voluntary hermit-like existence, the one comfort I really miss is congenial conversation with a kindred soul. One meets few gentlemen of refinement in this part of the country. Confidentially, I find Sheriff Dorgan and his aides almost incomprehensible much of the time. In the west, as you must have noticed, the beauty of the English language is rarely heard. Frontier folk seem to communicate in a patois all their own."

"Philistines abound," Doc agreed.

"I'll look forward to further friendly chats," said Haskin. "Now what was I on the point of asking a moment ago?" He stroked his brow. "Been rambling I'm afraid — denied intelligent conversation so long . . . "

"Before we digressed, you said 'by the way'," offered Doc.

"Ah, yes," said Haskin. "I was about to ask if you'd care for a spot of tea in a little while."

"Tea." Doc nodded approvingly. "Thoughtful of you, Haskin. And a pleasant change from jailhouse coffee."

"Earl Grey of course," said Haskin. "A friend in London keeps me supplied, dear soul that she is. Old lady-friend actually. Married to one of the banking and shipping Carringtons now, the elder son I believe. Ah, memories. Well, jolly good. Tea in an hour. Must get back to my current tome now."

"Shakespeare," Doc supposed.

"Milton," said Haskin.

At midnight, when Dorgan was alone in his office and wondering if he dared retire to his hotel room, a townman of his acquaintance knocked and entered.

"Bad news, Sheriff . . . "

"Just once," sighed Dorgan, "I'd

relish the chance for eight hours straight sleep. I was about to turn in, Arne, in hopes there'd be no more hullabaloos before sun-up. Pardon me, I should call you *Mister* Arne, right? I mean, now that you've hung out your shingle?"

"I'd like to think I'm still young Marcus to you," said Cluff City's youngest lawyer, helping himself to a chair. "You've known me since I was in my late teens and that was long before I graduated. We needn't stand on ceremony, Sheriff."

Dorgan nodded reminiscently while studying his visitor. He liked Marcus Arne, this neatly-attired, handsome-looking six-footer; rough though he was, he maintained a grudging respect for men of better education.

"Okay, Marcus, what's the bad news?"

"There's been a death," said Marcus. "It happened less than fifteen minutes ago."

"Oh, great." Dorgan grimaced irritably. "Two killin's in one night.

31

That's all I needed."

"Not a killing," frowned Marcus. "Not in the sense your mean. Death from natural causes. Doctor Colborn was in attendance when he died. I was there too. A seizure, the doctor said. He'd been expecting it." He shrugged sadly. "Well, he always was a heavy drinker and, according to Jim Colborn, too fond of rich foods. It was inevitable, but I'm sure many of us will miss him."

"You're tellin' me everything except the name of the latest stiff," complained Dorgan.

"Mister Queel," said Marcus.

"Old Barney?" winced Dorgan. "Hell. The old town won't seem the same. Quite a character he was."

"He had kin," Marcus reminded him. "A brother in Iowa."

"Schoolteacher, right?" prodded Dorgan. "Yeah, I remember. Barney bragged of him every so often — mostly when he was drunk. White sheep of the family. That's what he called his brother Marv. You were there when Barney cashed in?"

"He asked for me after he collapsed, after Jim Colborn was summoned," said Marcus. "He was still able to talk, wanted to remind me of the terms of his will, though he needn't have exerted himself. It's all legal and binding, every provision noted. I felt obliged to stay on while — Jim Colborn did his best to save him." Now, from his pockets, he produced a copy of the will and, to Dorgan's surprise, a ring of jingling keys. "These are duplicates to every key at the hotel. I have to direct you now, on behalf of the late Bernard Queel, to evict all occupants, be they resident or visitors, from the Queel Hotel forthwith. The building should then be locked up, sealed and protected from vandals or other intruders pending advice from the new owner.

"Forthwith?" blinked Dorgan.

"Meaning immediately," grinned Marcus.

"Hell's bells, boy, you know what that place is," Dorgan protested. "Little better than a cat-house."

"Let's say Mister Queel was none too particular about people renting accommodation at his establishment," shrugged Marcus. "Nevertheless he was *very* particular about what should happen after his demise — *immediately* after his demise. He imposed that condition on every guest, Sheriff. They were made to understand that, upon his death, they'd have to move out, and promptly, and they all agreed. So it shouldn't come as too great a shock to them. Do you wish to read the relevant clause?"

"No, damn it, just let me have those keys," grouched Dorgan. "Sam just started the graveyard shift. I'll find him and we'll get it done rightaway — just like Barney wanted. But those joy-girls and layabouts are gonna wail up a storm." As he got to his feet, he added, "And, speakin' of storm, you hear the wind blowin'?"

"It's a mean night," nodded the lawyer.

"A mean night for what Sam and me got to do," declared Dorgan.

Coincidentally, at this very moment, one of the nomadic Texans camped some distance east of Gomez County, was gloomily remarking,

"A real mean night, runt."

To this, the other Texan drawled agreement.

"Ain't that the truth."

Not for the first time in their many years of wandering, Larry Valentine and Stretch Emerson, sometimes referred to by frontier journalists, frontier lawmen and desperadoes as the Texas Trouble-Shooters, were cursing the perversity of frontier weather conditions.

2

What Are Friends For?

AT sundown it had seemed a good enough campsite, this brushy hogsback a few miles south of the Judson stage-trail. At sundown, however, the air had been still, no driving wind to bedevil the drifters, to assail their fire and scatter sparks that could ignite dry brush. Larry's sorrel and Stretch's pinto were shifting restlessly, nickering their disquiet. Had they possessed the power of speech, both animals would have echoed the taller Texan's mumbled assertion.

"We got to get the hell out of here."

"First thing we got to do . . . " began Larry.

"I'm doin' it," growled Stretch, and

he began smothering their fire with dirt.

While his partner forestalled what could have become an inferno, Larry Valentine busied himself with saddling their horses. He was three inches shorter than his six and a half feet tall sidekick, burly, broad-shouldered, deep-chested and ruggedly handsome, showing a three-day stubble that matched his dark-brown thatch. He wore, like Stretch, the rig favored by range riders of the Texas Panhandle country, the land of their birth. Their rig differed in only one respect; he packed one Colt to his partner's two, Stretch being ambidextrous with handguns. In the matter of personality, the contrast was more marked. He was the thinker of this much-traveled duo, the more nimble wit, the schemer when needs be. Even so, Woodville Eustace Emerson was as reliable, as loyal a sidekick as a much younger Larry could have wished for in the wild days of their first getting together; they had met at an enlistment centre when war was declared and had been companeros ever since.

Gangling, easy-going, guileless, but a formidable ally in time of crisis, Stretch tended to defer to his partner when decisions were called for. He was tow-haired and homely and his beanpole physique was sometimes deceptive, giving little hint of his prodigious strength. For the better part of two decades, he had been Larry's back-up in a hundred and one life or death encounters with the predators of the frontier, any kind of miscreant a duly-elected law officer could name, rustler, claim-jumpers, homicidal gunslingers, bank bandits, hold-up hordes preying on stagecoaches and the railroads — any kind.

At this moment, of course, their only adversary was the howling wind sweeping Central Colorado.

"Spotted a light earlier," Larry recalled.

"Yup," grunted Stretch, pointing north. "Thataway."

"Might be a homesteader's shack," suggested Larry. Their packrolls and saddlebags secured, their Winchesters sheathed, they stepped up to leather and guided their mounts down the north slope. "Well, whatever kind of shelter, we sure as hell need it."

"And who'd turn a couple peaceable hombres like us away," Stretch said optimistically, "on a night like this?"

Peaceable. That was the irony. In truth, the notorious outlaw-fighters had never sought fame and glory. When their wanderlust had lured them out of the Lone Star State at the end of the war, a futile quest had begun. They hadn't set out to make a name for themselves, to build a reputation. Their non-existent Utopia was a piece of territory where the only guns ever heard were those of hunters scoring on jackrabbit, quail or deer, where never a voice was raised in anger nor a jaw struck by a fist. They really *were* peace-loving, but peace had been denied them. Wherever they roamed, it always happened. Another fight not of their choosing, another clash with the lawless, another stranger in need, another malefactor to be exposed and defeated.

When it came to defeating desperadoes, they had notched up quite a score, much to the delight of newspapermen, if not to the approval of authority figures such as county sheriffs, town and Federal marshals, the Pinkerton Detective Agency and the U.S. Army. They were still winning, still succeeding where the law often failed, and had found to their grim amusement that authority figures resented their successes, were downright unappreciative in fact. But then it had to be conceded they were less than respectful of due process of law. Certainly they got results — in their own wild-swinging, gun-fast way.

Forty-five minutes after quitting the ridge, they were drawing closer to the source of the light glimpsed earlier. To their relief, it still showed bright, but Stretch was moved to wonder,

"Don't them folks never *sleep*?"

"Homestead was my first guess," said Larry. "Well, by damn, I was never so glad to be wrong. See the corrals?"

"Horse corrals," Stretch happily observed. "Big barn. Double-storied house. A spring, a root garden and chicken-coops. Doggone it, we found us a stage station! You know what that means?"

"Shelter for our critters, plenty spare beds," nodded Larry. "And good grub."

The hoofbeats of approaching horses were heard by people inside the house. A door opened as the wind-bedeviled riders crossed the trail and came on to the front yard. From the doorway, a squatly-built man gestured to the barn and called an invitation; after stabling their animals, they were welcome to come inside.

Some eight minutes later, the tall men were trading greetings with the two couples manning this outpost, the brothers Kermit and Hyram Smith and wives Lou and Maudie, elderly but durable comforters to teams, crews and passengers passing through the Nimbus Spring way station.

Why were these good folk still awake, though in bedroom attire? Kermit Smith's boil was the culprit, a big one right there on the back of his neck and giving him hell. It had come to a head and the women had made certain preparations calculated to relieve him of his agony. His spouse was ready with hot water and a poultice. Maudie had immersed a thin-bladed knife with a needle-sharp point in a glass of whiskey. But Kermit would hear no talk of surgery.

"The pain's a misery!" he groaned. "But no doc ever cut me in my whole life and I couldn't abide it now!"

"Nearest doc's at Cluff City, and that's a fair trace from here," Hyram remarked to the Texans.

"That boil's got to be lanced, Kermit," insisted Lou.

"So we can all get some sleep," sniffed Maudie.

"Just a little nick'll do it," Lou said cajolingly. "One tiny jab and it's all over. Poultice'll finish the job."

"Best way to be rid of the pain, Kermit," drawled Stretch, leaning over him to inspect the aching lump. Kermit was seated at the kitchen table, bowed forward, brow resting on his folded arms. And groaning louder now. "Plumb easy chore."

"No knife!" gasped Kermit.

Larry, after a critical appraisal of the boil, winked encouragingly at Hyram and the women and helped himself to the knife. He nodded to Stretch, who promptly crouched to wrap an arm about the sufferer's shoulders and plant a hand on his bowed head. Kermit wailed a protest, but was held fast with his affliction inviting Larry's attention. As Lou had promised, it required only a nick, just a gentle prod of the knife-point, to burst the boil. Kermit roared, Lou laid on the poultice and

43

made haste to secure it with plaster and, abruptly, the roars ceased. Shame-facedly, Kermit admitted,

"Feels better already."

"Told you, didn't I?" grinned Stretch, releasing him.

The patient's gratitude was boundless, and that went double for his spouse, brother and sister-in-law. It transpired Kermit wasn't a man to suffer in silence. This had been a five-day boil, agonizing for Kermit, almost as harrowing an ordeal for his kinfolk. Thus, a deft prod with a knife-point endeared the fiddlefoots to the Smiths of Nimbus Spring for all time. They were ushered to comfortable rooms, urged to sleep as late as they wished and assured of the hospitality of this place for an indefinite period.

"Stay on as long as you want, boys," were Hyram's final words. "Couple weeks, couple months. On the house. You're our guests. Won't cost us nothin'. Judson Line's pickin' up the tab."

For almost a month, the Texans had drifted the Colorado high country, content with each other's company, hunting and fishing at will. But they weren't hermits. They were gregarious and appreciative of this hospitality. Nimbus Spring was their idea of a fine hangout for flopping around, eating regularly and enjoying the lazy life until restlessness again assailed them.

★ ★ ★

By 9 a.m. of the next day, the Queel Hotel on Cluff City's main street, that double-storied, eighteen-roomed structure previously accommodating a cross-section of the local low-life, was empty, locked and under guard. The building was on Main's west side and a half-block from the sheriff's office and county jail, the austere building occupying the northwest corner of Main and Moredo. Lawmen would keep it under observation during the daylight hours and, from sundown to sun-up, patrol-walking deputies would include it on their beat, keeping a wary eye out for deadbeat intruders, vandals and the like. The last male occupant to depart had purloined the few items of value found in Room 13 on the second floor, once the resting place of the late Beau Mosser.

The all-important letter to the next-of-kin was mailed by Marcus Arne on his way to the county jail for another visit. Ralph Gibb, editor of the Bulletin, the county's only newspaper, had published a brief account of the murder of one gambler by another of his kind, and now Marcus was bent on offering his services. Ben Berry ushered the young lawyer into the cellblock after first warning him his offer would be refused. But Marcus had to verify that.

"Conduct your own defense, Mister Beaumont?" he protested. "That's too chancy. It's never wise for a defendant, especially when the charge is murder, a hanging offense, to rely on his own restricted knowledge of the law . . . "

"Thank you for your concern, young man." Doc gesturerd grandly. "You may leave now."

Bemused, Marcus peered through the bars at the prisoner. Doc was seated at a table in his shirtsleeves, writing up his notes, all the points he intended making, all the counters to the charge against which he would defend himself within twelve hours of the coming of the circuit-judge. To Marcus's contemplative eye, the cell was beginning to resemble the private office of a business executive; Doc was adept at creating atmosphere.

"It has been said . . . " began Marcus.

"An accused man who conducts his own defense has a fool for a client," nodded Doc. "Yes, I've heard it said, but my decision is final."

"Sure you aren't being over-confident?" frowned Marcus.

"Not at all," smiled Doc. "I am wrongly accused and therefore

47

determined to show up the addle-brained law officers of this shabby metropolis for the fools they undoubtedly are."

"You could antagonize the judge, however impartial he tries to be," warned Marcus. "Not to mention the jury."

"On the contrary," retorted Doc. "The judge will be most favorably impressed — and the jury in the palm of my hand. Go away, boy, you bother me."

A few days later, Arne's communication reached the schoolteacher of Purdyville, Iowa, was duly read and its import digested. Marvin Queel, with mixed feelings, re-read the letter to his family at suppertime and accurately assessed the reaction.

"We'll grieve for my brother, though you girls and your dear mother barely knew him, and we'll continue to be grateful to him," he declared. "For us, this bequest is — like a reprieve. We have so little money now, and chances of recovery of the Toliver Bank's funds are slim indeed."

"How much actual cash?" frowned his wife.

He consulted the letter again.

"Three thousand, six hundred and thirty-two dollars and twenty-five cents."

"Not a fortune, but so welcome," murmured Josephine.

"Well said, daughter," nodded Marvin. "More than I'd ever be able to save . . . "

"But certainly not a fortune," warned Flora. "So it must be used prudently, Marvin. We have to think of the future of these girls and make proper provision. A spending spree would be ill-advised, I believe."

"There's the property too," Prudence reminded them. "Papa owns a hotel now."

"The hotel is uppermost in my thoughts," said Marvin. "You and your sisters are mature enough — I trust — to comprehend Mister Arne's discreet remarks as to — uh — the kind of people accommodated there."

"I'd say Mister Arne made it obvious — in his discreet way," chuckled Angeline.

"Really, child," chided Flora.

"Anyway, we needn't be embarrassed," the youngest daughter suggested. "Mister Arne has assured Papa the place has been emptied, all unsavory guests expelled."

"Your mother and I have to consider an important question now," said Marvin. "Where does our future lie? On the one hand, Purdyville is a tranquil town and we have friends here. I could continue to teach and the cash bequest could be regarded as rental of this home for a considerable period. But . . . " He traded glances with his wife, "is that enough?"

"If we wish to see our daughters make good marriages, I can't see it happening in Purdyville," was her answer. "Eligible young men — with prospects — aren't exactly plentiful here."

"On the other hand," Marvin continued, "Cluff City is a town the like of which we've never known. Its economy is dependent on mining and the raising of cattle. Mister Arne describes it as a town with a future, a place that will certainly grow and prosper. In its present state, however, it is — I suppose turbulent is the word."

"Rough frontier town," Ruth said thoughtfully.

"And exciting," guessed Angeline, her eyes sparkling.

"If we resettled in Cluff City to run the hotel as a respectable house, it could become our oasis in a manner of speaking," Marvin pointed out. "Our place of business, but catering only to people acceptable to us. After all, the entire population can't be unruly. In the wildest towns, such as Dodge City, Tombstone and Wichita, I'm sure there are decent, God-fearing folk still going to church, still living respectable lives. Denver is now a city. But, in its

51

early years, I'm told it was far from peaceful."

"My dear, I believe we could achieve something in Cluff City," Flora said firmly. "The Queel family could become a steadying influence. Isn't that the effect we've had on Purdyville? The few disreputable men of this community are over-awed by our daughters and by us. The girls have never been molested or even accosted. That surly drunkard, Jake Hollis, for instance, never fails to raise his hat. Would I sound self-righteous were I to suggest Cluff City *needs* us?"

"I think Mother's absolutely right," smiled Prudence. "We really could achieve something."

"Eighteen rooms, four bathrooms, the inevitable bar, a dining room and — all other facilities," mused Marvin. "My first step would be to convert the bar to two bedrooms, make it a twenty-room hotel. I never could read Bernard's mind, but I wonder if

— he *meant* for us to resettle in Cluff City."

"We wouldn't need to hire staff, not at first," Flora said encouragingly. "Our daughters are so *capable*, Marvin. We can share the cooking chores, the room cleaning, the waiting on tables. And you, so educated, so adaptable, could easily fill the role of hotel manager. Marvin, dear, five healthy women and a man of culture and imagination could make the Queel Hotel the most refined establishment in Cluff City!"

"It's a *wonderful* idea," enthused Ruth.

"Just wonderful," agreed Josephine.

"Well, the lawyer did enclose a bank draft, five hundred dollars to meet immediate expenses," remarked Marvin, trading smiles with his wife. "It seems the conference is over and the decision unanimous. Win or lose, the Queels of Iowa are to become the Queels of Colorado."

"I'm glad this house was rented furnished," declared Flora. "What personal effects can't be carried with us can be shipped freighted to our destination."

"One wagonload," Josephine estimated.

"Can we travel some of the way by railroad?" begged Ruth.

"As far as possible," nodded her father. "But I expect we'll finish our journey by stagecoach." He showed his loved ones a brave grin. "I'll wire Mister Arne right after supper and make some enquiries at the stage depot."

"Do that," urged Flora. "And — who knows? We could be on our way in just a couple of days."

★ ★ ★

Around 9 o'clock next morning, Ed Chilson's partner returned to the log shacks of the Grand Venture Mine's headquarters in the Sierra Rojo. For a week, the lean and venal Greg Javert had been taking a turn at reconnoitering the many claims of the high country, scouting, checking prospects, but from a safe distance and always from concealment; the Grand Venture rogue-pack relied heavily on telescopes and fieldglasses.

When Javert reined up and dismounted in the open area between the shaftheads and the cabin he shared with his partner, Chilson, Wynant and two other men were taking their ease in a patch of shade. A grin creased his saturnine visage as he ambled across to join them.

"Supplies run out?" drawled Wynant.

"Good to see you, Greg," nodded Chilson. "You're looking weary."

"And feeling hungry," said Javert, hunkering beside him. "Used up the last of my provisions mid-afternoon yesterday." He helped himself to a cigar from Chilson's vest pocket. "And had my last smoke around midnight. But it was worth the effort, this little look-around."

Chilson gave him a light and asked eagerly,

"Anybody caching the good stuff?"

"Hammond Mine," Javert reported. "The Lucky Spade too. They'll be our next unwilling suppliers. Hammond has only three men. There are five working the Lucky Spade. Easy pickings, Ed. We can take 'em any time you're ready."

"We'll give it a couple days," decided Chilson. "The more time we allow 'em, the bigger the take."

"Everything quiet here?" asked Javert.

"Here, sure," said Chilson, trading grins with Wynant. "But a little excitement in town a while back. Wait till you hear this, friend. We can stop fretting about Mosser. He's through blackmailing us. No more handouts to that sonofabitch."

"How'd you scare him off?" demanded Javert.

"Didn't scare him off," chuckled Cilson. "*Finished* him off. Milt took care of him for us. You sentimental, Greg? Like to put flowers on his grave? That's where he ended up. In the Cluff

56

City cemetery. Greg . . . " He grasped Javert's arm. "What's the matter with you?"

"Don't tell us you're gonna mourn Mosser," leered Wynant.

"Mosser's *dead*?" gasped Javert. He was suddenly haggard, sweat beading on his brow, trickling into his haunted eyes. "Damn it, that means we have to quit, pull out, make tracks!"

"Take it easy," growled Chilson. "It was all handled neatly."

"Real slick job," one of the other men commented.

"No chance the law'll come lookin' for me," Wynant assured Javert. "Stranger in town, a tinhorn name of Beaumont, made it easy for me. He got in a ruckus with Mosser."

"Mosser called him out," explained Chilson. "They traded shots in the alley back of the Siren Saloon while Milt was staked out with Mosser in his sights. One in the back, and they're blaming Beaumont for it. He'll hang for the killing — so our troubles are over. Not another dime of our money will Mosser see."

"Too dead to care," drawled Wynant.

"You don't understand!" Javert gesticulated wildly. "He kept an ace up his sleeve! We're all gallows-bait now — or are you forgetting the two we gunned down when we looted the Jackson Mine a couple of months back . . . ?"

"Will you, for the love of Mike, stop raving and make sense?" scowled Chilson.

"All right, listen to me," breathed Javert. "The night I started this scouting expedition, I stopped by the county seat for a few things I needed. That's the last time I saw Mosser alive. And we talked."

"Same night you took off?" frowned Wynant. "That'd be the night before I downed him."

"He was drunk and talkative — and very glad to see me," said Javert. "Fortunately nobody else heard, not that it makes any difference now. Oh, hell! He told me . . . !"

"Simmer down," ordered Chilson. "*What* did he tell you?"

"He bragged of — having insurance," muttered Javert. "Warned me — we'd have to keep on paying for his silence and forget . . . " His face contorted, "forget any fool notion we might have — such as harming him in any way — or trying to kill him. If that happens, he said, Sheriff Dorgan will damn soon know who raided the Jacksons and the other claims. He put it all on paper, Ed, sealed it and wrote Dorgan's name on it. To be opened in the event of his death. Don't you see? We're all through! There's no hope for us!"

"It was a bluff," insisted Chilson. "He was bragging drunk, you said."

"I don't believe he was bluffing," said Javert. "He told me the envelope was hidden in his room."

"Not left at the post office," grinned Chilson. "Hidden in his room. Stop worrying, Greg. Can't you see it *was* a bluff? If he wanted it delivered to

Dorgan, why would he hide it? He'd more likely leave it with a lawyer or at the postal telegraph."

"I'm responsible," fretted Javert. "I blame myself, Ed. I should've come straight back here and talked it over with you. The hell of it is I had no idea this would happen, no idea you'd make such a move against Mosser."

"It was too good a chance to pass up," shrugged Chilson. "All it took was one bullet. Now Mosser's gone and this dude Beaumont will hang and Dorgan'll be none the wiser. Be reasonable, Greg. If there was such a letter, we wouldn't be here now. A minute after reading it, Dorgan would have deputized a posse and come out here to arrest the whole outfit."

"I wish I was as sure as you," Javert retorted. "There'll be no peace for me till I find and burn it. My responsibility, my mistake, and I'll make up for it. I have to get into that room, search it till I . . . "

"Tip your hand?" challenged Chilson.

"Forget it. By now, somebody else is renting that room. Not a hotel room in Cluff City stays vacant long."

"You ain't heard?" Another man spoke up, a flat-nosed felon known only as Curly. "Mosser used to bunk at old Barney Queel's place. Room Thirteen, second floor. I know that for a fact."

"What's your point?" prodded Chilson.

"So you *ain't* heard," shrugged Curly. "Queel Hotel's empty. I got it from the barkeep at the Pay Ore Saloon. When old Barney died, seems he left a will. Hotel belongs to his brother now. Dorgan flushed the place out, locked it up till the new owner gets here. Meantime, nobody gets in."

"*I'll* get in," declared Javert. "I *have* to. It's my responsibility."

"Now, Greg . . . " began Chilson.

"Think of it," said Javert, trembling again, "if that letter fell into Dorgan's hands, we'd all hang!"

"That won't happen," soothed Chilson.

"Oh, hell!" Javert bowed his head. "It's in that room — somewhere — still hidden, otherwise Dorgan would be hounding us now. And, if it's found by anybody else . . . !"

"There's no letter," insisted Chilson. "Even if there was, it could stay hidden for years."

"Can't take that chance," mumbled Javert. "Tonight. Yes, this very night, I'll search the room, every inch of it."

★ ★ ★

At the Nimbus Spring station, 1.15 p.m. of this same day, two contented Texans smoked their after-lunch cigarettes in caneback chairs on the porch and traded friendly talk with their amiable host. No longer in pain, Kermit Smith nevertheless retained painful memories. That had been some boil; he never stopped thanking Surgeon Valentine and Assistant-Surgeon Emerson. An eastbound stage had rolled in for lunch and a team-switch and had departed on schedule. Now, before trudging inside to take a nap, Kermit slid a folded newspaper from under his arm and tossed it to Larry's lap.

"Paper from Cluff City, if you're a readin' man. Eric, the shotgun guard, left it behind."

Stretch slumped low in his chair and, through half-closed eyes, admired the scenery visible from the porch, still relishing the tranquility of this region. Larry worked his quirley to the side of his mouth, unfolded the Gomez County Bulletin and began reading. He was up to page three when he broke the silence.

"Too good to last," he complained.

"Howzat again?" prodded Stretch.

"Can't hang around here no more," Larry said regretfully. "We're gonna have to saddle up and head for Cluff City."

"Why so?" demanded Stretch.

"He needs help," said Larry. "They got him waitin' trial for murder in the county jail. Some hombre name of Mosser got backshot and they're claimin' he did it."

"Who's he?"

"Doc Beaumont."

"So they done arrested the wrong gun. No way Doc'd draw bead on a man's back. Ain't his style."

"You know it, I know it and Doc knows it, but the county sheriff calls it murder and claims Doc's the one."

"I guess — uh — we better do somethin' about that. But what?"

"We'll fret about that when we make Cluff City." Larry discarded the paper. "So that's it. Time to adios the Smiths."

The brothers and their wives were disappointed their guests were obliged to cut short their stay at the switch station, but wished them easy riding to their destination and offered directions, uncomplicated directions; to make Cluff City, the next stage stop west, any time tomorrow morning, they need only follow the trail. They were made promise to stop by again when their business at Cluff City was finished. They vowed to do that and, good-humoredly, Larry made Kermit an offer.

"You grow another boil any time from here on, just stay patient. We'll tend it for you on our way back."

By the time they were saddled up and ready to move out, the wives had packed a gunnysack with provisions for their journey, more than enough for the two meals they would eat between here and their destination, tonight's supper, tomorrow morning's breakfast.

"We're sure gonna eat hearty," Stretch gleefully commented.

"Got to keep your strength up," insisted Maudie.

Warmed by the Smiths' Godspeed, the tall men waved farewell and took to the trail west. Their sojourn at Nimbus Spring had been brief but pleasant.

Now, because an old cohort of theirs had gotten himself in trouble, there was no way they could stay out of it. Had Nimbus Springs been a thousand miles from the Gomez County jail, they would still have felt compelled to make this journey. They liked Doc. He didn't like them, didn't approve of them at all, but this was of minor importance. Old debts should never be forgotten.

"We owe him," remarked Stretch. "He's saved our hides a time or two."

"We'll always owe Doc," nodded Larry.

"Mind now, *we've* saved *his* hide many a time," frowned Stretch.

"Uh huh," shrugged Larry. "But what're friends for?"

"Cattle and gold-minin' is what keeps Cluff City goin', Hyram told me," recalled Stretch. "Gonna be plenty rough hombres at Cluff, runt. Same kind we always tangle with."

"Not this time," Larry said firmly. "We can't do nothin' for Doc if we end up in the same calaboose. So we're gonna keep our noses clean. No rough stuff, amigo. Unless some hothead gets a fool notion Doc ought to be lynched."

3

Unexpected Welcome

1.45 of the following morning, while Larry and Stretch were in deep sleep at their camp by the stage trail, some but not all of Cluff City's saloons had closed for business. In the big town, certain parties slumbered as deeply as the fiddlefoots destined to arrive around 10 a.m.

Sheriff Jerry Dorgan, grateful the sundown to midnight period had been unmarred by violent incident, was dead to the world in his hotel room. Deputy Sam Tragg, having taken the sundown to midnight patrol, had been deep in slumber this past hour on the law office couch. In the end cell of the jailhouse, turnkey Theo Haskin's lamp still glowed; as well as being a bookworm, the Englishman was somewhat of an insomniac. Doc Beaumont, still the jail's only inmate, had retired to his bunk before 10 p.m., planning on sleeping till awakened for breakfast by his jailer-friend who behaved more as a butler and confidant than as a jailer. The youthful Deputy Ben Berry was walking the graveyard shift and the very anxious Greg Javert climbing the firestairs leading up from the alley behind the Queel Hotel to its second floor gallery.

Until he approached the locked-up hotel by way of the back alley, young Ben's mind was wandering. He was at that age after all, the age at which, whether or not it be springtime, a young man's thoughts are apt to turn to something fancy. Unlike his boss and the elder deputy, Ben was averse to the idea of permanent bachelorhood.

He was not yet acquainted with one of Cluff City's prettier spinsters, Harriet, daughter of baker Clem Primble, but was thinking of doing something about that. A mind-picture of the girl's comely face was conjured up as he drew closer to the hotel. This sure was fine weather for the time of year, the sky so full of winking stars that he instinctively raised his face to admire them. Only then did he glimpse the shadowy figure moving along the gallery.

The deputy's shouted challenge startled Javert, whose reaction was impulsive and swift. His Colt was out and leveled before Ben could finish his challenge.

"Hey, you up there! What . . . ?"

He wasn't given time to cock his shotgun, much less raise it. He heard the shot and, at the same moment, was shoved off-balance by the impact of the bullet creasing his left arm. To the opposite wall he reeled, a brick wall struck by his head when his legs failed him. That impact, as powerful as the impact of the bullet, plunged him into oblivion.

Javert cursed in frustration, his ears bedeviled by the sound of yelled questions from Main Street and stumbling footsteps.

'Move fast,' he warned himself. 'You can't afford to be sighted — recognized!'

He holstered his six-gun, retreated to the firestairs and descended to the alley in frantic haste. He was lost from view in the gloom, making for the side street where his horse was tied, when two minehands a mite the worse for booze lurched into the back alley and discovered the prone man.

Minutes later, Tragg's sleep was broken by a pounding on the locked street-door of the law office. He growled complaints as he lit a lamp and padded across the office in his stockinged feet.

"Who's out there — and the hell with you whoever you are?"

"We found the young feller, the young deputy, in the alley back of the Queel place," came the urgent reply. "Dunno if he's dead or alive. Didn't nobody else hear the shot?"

"Theo!" roared Tragg.

"Here," said Haskin, appearing in

71

the cellblock entrance. "They're right, Deputy Tragg. There was a shot. I heard it."

"You know the routine," muttered Tragg, as he began dressing. "Lock the door after me. Don't open up for anybody but me, the boss or . . . "

"Any reputable citizen," nodded Haskin. "Right you are, old chap. Not to worry. I'm familiar with the procedure."

Tragg finished dressing, took a shotgun from the rack, unlocked the door and moved out, ordering the fast-sobering minehands to lead him to his fallen colleague. Haskin re-secured the door, left the lamp burning and moved back into the jail to find his new friend stirring.

Propped up on an elbow, knuckling at his eyes, Doc mumbled,

"What now? I need eight hours of sleep, confound it."

"I'm most dreadfully sorry, Beaumont," the jailer apologized. "You needn't concern yourself. Do go back to sleep."

"That's not an answer," chided Doc.

"A shooting," said Haskin. "One of the deputies. I've no idea how serious . . . "

"Which deputy?" asked Doc. "The ugly one, or the boy?"

"Actually, Ben Berry is in his early twenties," said Haskin. "Rather callow, but a good lad. Tragg is investigating."

"I've nothing against the boy, callow though he is," frowned Doc. "Let's hope it's not a fatal wound. Thunderation, Haskin, there's a homicidal gunman on the loose in this town, and he's trigger-happy. Might be the same fellow who slew the man *I'm* supposed to have shot." He lowered his head to his pillow. "No doubt in my mind, Haskin. He was somewhere behind me. When I fired over Mosser's head, the real killer fired at his back. The two shots merged as one."

"Remarkable timing, wouldn't you say?" suggested Haskin.

"Freak luck more likely," grunted Doc.

When young Ben regained consciousness, his vision was fuzzy and his head throbbing. It took him a few moments to get everything into focus, and then he recognized this room and the three men hovering over him. He was on Dr Emil Schubert's operating table; also present were the other two-thirds of the local law.

"What happened, kid?" growled Tragg.

"No questions," chided Schubert. "He oughtn't be questioned yet."

"Don't try to talk, young Ben," frowned Dorgan. "Just tell us who shot you."

"Save your strength, young feller," urged Schubert.

Ben groaned and forced his eyes wide open.

"Make up your minds," he begged.

"Can you see this?" asked Schubert.

"Yeah," grunted Ben. "It's your finger. Why are you shaking it at me?"

"It's not shaking," said Schubert,

turning to Dorgan. "Concussion, but not too serious. Still, with that and the arm-wound, he's in no shape for duty, needs a couple of days rest at least. All right, I'll let him talk, but don't badger him."

"Not — hurt bad?" Ben asked hopefully.

"Shallow crease, left arm," offered Tragg. "We figured you were knocked against the wall across the alley from the Queel Hotel, hit it head-first. You hear what Doc said? You're gonna be fine."

"You sight the man who shot you?" prodded Dorgan.

"He was just a shadow," mumbled Ben. "Second floor gallery — that's where he was when I spotted him. I hollered and — wham! Heard him shoot at me and — it was like I got licked by a mule!"

"Yeah, okay, that's enough," soothed Dorgan. "Plain enough, Sam. He surprised some no-account lookin' for a free bed. The marauder took fright when those minehands came a'runnin' from the street. They didn't see anybody?"

"He was too fast on his feet," said Tragg.

"You take Ben home, then get on back to sleep," ordered Dorgan. "How many shotguns d'you have there? Never mind. I'll take this one and finish the graveyard shift. Can't ask you to, Sam. The way you look, you and Ben mightn't make it to his boarding house."

"We'll make it," shrugged Tragg. "All right now, you brave law officer you, let's get you on your feet."

"Young feller's first gunshot wound — his baptism by fire," the medico sombrely remarked. "They'll regret their decision, mark my words."

"Who?" frowned Dorgan, helping himself to a shotgun.

"Old Queel's brother and family, the gentlefolk from Iowa he always bragged about," grouched Schubert. "What a tragedy this town is still untamed.

The good Lord knows it's no place for a schoolteacher getting into the hotel business."

"Does all of Cluff City know Barney's kin're headed our way?" complained Dorgan.

"Why *wouldn't* everybody know?" challenged Schubert. "Our resident gossip-monger, the editor of our newspaper, lost no time spreading the word. It wasn't supposed to be a secret anyway, was it?"

"I guess not," said Dorgan. "Well, maybe they'll stay or maybe they'll spook and head back to Iowa. Up to them. Meanwhile, the hotel still needs guardin' — in case some deadbeat breaks in, feels cold and lights a fire where there's no fireplace and burns the whole place down."

By 9.50 a.m. this day, at which time the Texans were idling their mounts into Main Street to seek a livery stable, Dorgan was beginning to feel slightly more awake. A shave and bath had refreshed him to some extent and, with his senior deputy, he had accounted for several cups of black coffee. Tragg was at the office stove again now, brewing another potful.

At the stable of their choice, the Billings Barn, the tall strangers easily recognized the thoroughbred in the end stall.

"Doc's," Stretch said emphatically.

"Sure enough," agreed Larry dropping his voice. "But try to remember not to call him that. You know how he is. He don't appreciate for folks to know . . . "

"Oh, sure," nodded Stretch.

While offsaddling, Larry put a question to the stablehand, a wiry old timer with a ready grin, Willy Dobbs by name.

"Nearest hotel to the county jail? That'll be the Queel Hotel, son, but you got no chance of checkin' in there."

"Full up," guessed Stretch.

"Closed up, locked up," grinned Dobbs. "Want to hear somethin' funny? Listen, this is a real rib-tickler. That used to be old Barney Queel's place, and he wasn't much particular who hung out there. It wasn't much better'n a cat-house . . . "

"You comin' to the funny part?" prodded Larry.

"Barney up and died and damned if he didn't will the hotel to his high-falutin' brother, a schoolteacher no less," cackled the stablehand. "And now this gent, Mister Marvin Queel from Iowa, he's comin' to Cluff with his fine wife and daughters, see? They used to be the most high-toned family in Purdyville, Iowa, but they'll be movin' into a bawdy house!"

At that point, a good-looking townman entered the barn and reprimanded Dobbs.

"That isn't funny at all, Willy. And now, instead of gossiping at these strangers, will you kindly saddle a good animal for me? I have business at the Scudder and Pitney Mine."

"C'mon now, young Marcus, you just *know* it's funny," leered Dobbs, after which he imparted further information to the strangers. "This here buck that I've knowed since he was a sprig is Marcus Arne. He was old Barney's lawyer and it was him sent for the Iowa folks."

"I didn't send for them," Marcus said testily. "I advised them of the bequest. The decision to come to Cluff City was theirs." He appealed to the Texans. "Pay no attention to Willy. He has a big mouth and a perverted sense of humor. Excuse me. Thanks to Willy's big mouth, you know who I am, but you have the advantage of me."

"Lawrence," offered Larry.

"Woodville," said Stretch.

"Mister Lawrence, Mister Woodville, welcome to Cluff City," nodded Marcus. "Willy, what about my horse?"

"Go ahead, Willy," urged Stretch. "Saddle up for this gent. We'll tend to our own critters."

Nothing more was said until the tall men had stashed their saddles and gear and Marcus was leading a saddled dun colt from the barn. They ambled out after him. About to raise boot to stirrup, he paused to the touch of Larry's hand on his shoulder.

"Got a minute, Mister Arne, before you ride out?"

"Something I can do for you?" asked Marcus.

"Just a question," said Larry. "Friend of ours — name of Beaumont . . . "

"To be tried for murder," nodded Marcus.

"He's the one," said Larry. "My partner and me, we're wonderin' if you're the lawyer he hired."

"Mister Beaumont seems allergic to lawyers," Marcus said ruefully. "He's determined to plead his own case. I offered my services, but he's adamant, and I can't talk him out of it." He frowned curiously. "No offense, but are you really friends of his? I mean, such an articulate, highly educated gentleman?"

"That's our ol' buddy," grinned Stretch. "Plumb educated. Real quality."

"I know what you're thinkin'," Larry assured Marcus.

"I don't mean to offend . . . " began Marcus.

"Relax," soothed Larry. "We ain't sore. You see, it's this way. Our trails've crossed a time or two."

"Times when we had to fight our way out of gun-trouble, us and him," confided Stretch. "Anytime he sided us, he was mighty reliable."

"But he always ended up cussin' us out," said Larry. "We admire him a lot — only *he* don't much admire *us*."

"But we don't mind," Stretch hastened to assure the bemused lawyer.

"Just one of those things, you know?" drawled Larry. "It don't much matter, him not likin' us I mean. If he's around when we're in trouble, he always sides us."

"And vice versa," guessed Marcus.

"Howzat again?" frowned Stretch.

"You'd do the same for him," nodded Marcus. "Interesting. Complete opposites. Nothing in common — except a rare kind of loyalty."

"You could put it that way," said Larry. "So no lawyer, huh? Too bad. Judge mightn't take kindly to Vince's palaverin'. Might be he'll do himself more harm than good."

"If you have any influence with him at all, try to change his mind," advised Marcus, as he mounted the dun. "I'm not trying to drum up trade, you understand. He has another choice, the third attorney of this territory, Emmett O'Hare."

"We'll remember," said Larry. "Much obliged."

After the lawyer had ridden out, the strangers moved along Main in search of the sheriff's office and county jail. It didn't take them long to confirm the stablehand's words. The Queel establishment certainly was the hotel closest the headquarters of the local law. They studied the building casually and kept walking. Reaching their destination, they climbed to the porch.

Dorgan and Tragg traded glances as the tall men appeared in the open doorway, then eyed them expectantly. Determined to dodge conflict with the lawmen, they looked to their manners.

"Mornin'," Larry greeted them. "Take it kindly if you'd let us visit a prisoner name of Beaumont."

"Doc Beaumont," offered Stretch.

Larry winced irritably and growled a rebuke.

"There you go again."

"Sorry." Stretch also winced. "I keep gettin' it wrong. Should've said Duke Beaumont."

"He's the one," nodded Larry.

"Who's askin'?" drawled Dorgan.

"Yeah," grunted Tragg. "Who?"

"I'm Lawrence," said Larry. "He's Woodville."

"Well, sure," said Dorgan. "Lawrence Valentine and Woodville Emerson, usually called Stretch." He grinned and Larry was at once taken aback. A cold, mirthless grin would have seemed appropriate, more indicative of the unsociable attitude maintained by most frontier lawmen. But Dorgan's grin was amiable. Tragg also was showing them a similar grin. "Glad to see you jaspers."

"Yeah," nodded Tragg. "Welcome to Cluff City."

"Here to see Beaumont you say?" prodded Dorgan. "You acquainted with that high-falutin' tinhorn?"

"Known him quite a time," said Larry. "He ain't real partial to us, but we like him fine."

"That don't make a whole lot of sense," remarked Dorgan.

"Couple hassles we got mixed into, him and us," explained Larry.

"Must be three or four times we've had him sidin' us," corrected Stretch. "Maybe five or six. But who keeps count?"

"We owe him," Larry pointed out. "Like to help him if we can. Anything for a friend, you know?" He slipped his holster-throng and began unstrapping his shellbelt. "Okay if we talk to him."

"I know you wouldn't be fool enough to try bustin' him out of my jail, Valentine," said Dorgan. "Listen, if you're all that set on helpin' him, there's only one way. We're holdin' him for murder . . . "

"We read of it," said Stretch. "And we don't believe he did it. Back-shootin' just ain't his style."

"Best thing you can do for him, if you like him all that much, is talk him into hirin' a lawyer," declared Dorgan.

"He's got this fool notion of defendin' himself," offered Tragg.

"I've heard Judge Spalding say it many a time," warned Dorgan. "It's never smart for a defendant to fight his own case."

"We hears about that," frowned Larry, "from a young hombre name of Arne."

"So you know what he's up against," said Dorgan. "Let 'em in, Sam."

The Texans hung their sidearms on the gunrack. To their surprise, the deputy did not search them for concealed weapons before ushering them into the jailhouse.

"Stay as long as you like," drawled Tragg, retreating across the threshold.

"Actin' might friendly, these badge-toters," Stretch muttered quietly. "Makes me plumb nervous."

"They're friendly," agreed Larry. "And I'm wonderin' why."

As they trudged the passage to the occupied cell, the end cell opened and the jailer emerged to size them up. They nodded to him, then turned to aim greetings at Doc, who at once turned red and waxed wrathful.

"What in thunderation are *you two* doing here?"

"Howdy," grinned Stretch. "We're glad to see you too, Vince ol' buddy."

"Don't Vince old buddy me!" stormed Doc, rising and pointing toward the office. "Get out of my sight this instant! Of all times — the one time you could do the most damage — you have the gall to intrude!"

"Only stopped to help," soothed Larry. "Keep your silk shirt on, doggone it. You got yourself in a mess of trouble and we're here to pull you out of it, if we can."

"I say, steady on, Beaumont old chap," protested Haskin. "I mean, if they really wish to aid you in your predicament, surely you should . . . "

"You don't understand, Haskin!" fumed Doc. "They are heavy-handed, bull-headed meddlers, trouble-shooters, vagabonds of low intellect and they are incapable of finesse, of tact, of discretion. For me to accept their help would be disastrous!" He glowered at the abashed Texans. "And I forbid you to show your uncouth faces in the county courthouse when I stand trial! You'd be bound to antagonize the judge. It will be my day of triumph and, confound you, I'll not permit you to make a shambles of the proceedings. This is an order! You will, as of this very moment, *butt out*!"

"Think he's mad at us?" asked Stretch.

"Just a mite fazed," opined Larry. "Ain't every day he gets nailed for murder." He tried again. "Look, amigo, if there's anything we can do . . . "

"Out!" gasped Doc.

"We'll be around," shrugged Larry, "if you change your mind."

"*Don't* be around!" raged Doc. "Begone! Get out of town! Better still, get out of Colorado! I'll not tolerate your bungling interference in my affairs, and that's final!"

"Sounds like he means it," suggested Stretch.

"Ain't that the truth," agreed Larry. "Well, okay, Vince, have it your way. But we'll still be around."

He nudged Stretch. They retreated along the passage to rejoin the lawmen. Tragg shut the cellblock door and invited them to be seated. They noted the street-door had been closed and locked. They also noted the bottle and four glasses on Dorgan's desk and the affable grin on Dorgan's face.

"Good bourbon," the sheriff said encouragingly. "Sam'll be barkeep. Not too early in the day for you? He's Sam Tragg, my senior deputy. Call him Sam. And I'm Jerry to my friends. Tell me, Larry, were you able to change Beaumont's mind about . . . ?"

"Didn't get time," frowned Larry. "All he did was bawl us out."

Seated, the Texans watched Tragg pour generous shots. They didn't trade wondering glances, but the wonderment persisted. Rarely could lawmen, any lawmen anywhere, unsettle them; it usually worked the other way around. To their jaundiced eyes, Sheriff Dorgan and his deputy seemed out of character. Since when did peace officers accord them such hospitality, ply them with good booze? They made to fish out their makings. Dorgan forestalled that move by offering cigars. They accepted bourbon and cigars and a light from Tragg, after which Stretch warily enquired.

"You sure you ain't mistakin' us for two other hombres?"

Dorgan chuckled good-humoredly.

"C'mon now, Stretch," he drawled. "You and your partner are the only two of your kind. And we're glad you're here. Right, Sam?"

"Right," grinned Tragg, raising his glass in a salute. "Here's lookin' at you, boys."

"Glad we're here, huh?" challenged Larry. "Listen, thanks for the cheer. If you want to be sociable, that's fine by us, but you must've guessed we can't butt out of Beaumont's trouble."

"Got your heart set on a little independent detective work," guessed Dorgan. "Well, you hear anybody objectin'? Dig all you want and welcome, just so long as you cause no — uh — disturbance of the peace. And here's an idea. As temporary deputy sheriffs of Gomez County, you'd be entitled to ask questions anywhere you please. You'd be showin' badges and those badges stand for authority, give you a handy edge . . . "

"So that's it," Larry observed with a wry grin. Stretch, "for the glad hands and the booze and the friendly smiles."

"Jerry, I'm bettin' you hold a fat file on us," said Larry. "You recognized us right off. You know all about us, and how we operate, so you know how we feel about wearin' tin stars."

"Nervous is how we'd feel," declared Stretch. "Thanks a lot, but no thanks."

"Jerry and me got confidence in you," offered Tragg. "We ain't soreheads. Nobody ever heard us gripin' about the Lone Star Trouble-Shooters. You've done . . . " He frowned into his whiskey, "you've done good things."

"You play rough, but get results," Dorgan complimented them. "I know you've locked horns with many a law officer, but I don't hold that against you."

"We ain't grudge-toters," Tragg assured them.

"You've licked every thief and killer

you ever tangled with and, for that, we admire you," said Dorgan. "That's no bull, boys. We mean it."

"Comes straight from the heart," said Tragg, clasping hand to chest.

"I'm all shook up," scoffed Stretch.

"Have a heart," wheedled Tragg. "What'll it cost you to listen to Jerry's deal while you're drinkin' his good booze and smokin' them fine cigars?"

"I'm short-handed," complained Dorgan. "Havin' a killer in my jail is the least of my worries. I got other worries and they're gettin' bigger. For one thing, I'm responsible for protecting the estate of the late Barney Queel, meanin' an empty hotel that deadbeats keep tryin' to bust into. Barney's kinfolks're on their way here to re-open the place but, until then, it has to be guarded. One jackass, challenged by my other deputy, took a shot at him and vamoosed . . . "

"So we're one deputy down," explained Tragg. "He wasn't hurt bad, be back on the job in a couple days, but meanwhile we got more chores than we can handle."

"Situation's gettin' desperate," frowned Dorgan. "Cluff City — well — you can see what kind of town it is. Where you got miners and cattlemen in the same territory, you got trouble and plenty of it. One ruckus after another in the saloons, wild brawls, gunplay and the righteous citizens on my back to keep the town peaceful. Just policin' the county seat is trouble enough, but we got worse."

"Gold thieves hittin' the Sierra Rojo mines," said Tragg.

"Uh huh," grunted Larry. "Hijackin' shipments on their way to the stamp-mills."

"Not this bunch," grouched Dorgan. "They mount raids on the mines — and they're trigger-happy."

"Masked raiders swoopin' down on the claims of lone-wolf prospectors," said Dorgan, "as well as the big minin' companies."

Minehands try to defend 'emselves,

but they're always outnumbered," muttered Tragg.

"A sizeable gang," nodded Dorgan. "Well-organized. Well-armed. And, in those mountains, it's too damn easy for 'em to kill their tracks."

"On account of the Ramblin' Rattlesnake," interjected Tragg.

"The what?" blinked Larry.

"Ramblin' Rattlesnake Creek." Tragg elaborated. "It runs every whichaway through the high country."

"Shallow most of the way," sighed Dorgan. "Party of riders can travel it for miles. And who can tag horse-tracks through water? The gold-thieves never had it so good and, stuck here in town most of the time, what can I do? I got the mayor and his councilmen friends hammerin' at me to keep Cluff City's rowdies pinned down and the mineowners demandin' protection in the mountains. Larry, you're lookin' at all the law there is."

"Just Jerry and me," said Tragg.

"The jailer's reliable enough," Dorgan

conceded. "But that's all he is. Just a jailer. I got a need and you two could help, so what d'you say?"

Larry rejected the plea, but diplomatically.

"If things were different, you wouldn't be wantin' to depute us," he pointed out. "You'd be frettin' up a storm wonderin' how many fights we'd get prodded into, wonderin' if your calaboose is big enough to hold all the extra trade. And you wouldn't breathe easy till we quit town."

"Got to admit you're right about that," shrugged Dorgan.

"Pin stars on us and we'd be targets for every hothead minehand and cowpoke in this territory," stressed Larry. "Too many smart-alecks know us, too many fools packin' a hair-trigger hogleg and hankerin' to make a name for 'emselves."

"That's what the matter is," grumbled Stretch.

"So no badges," said Larry, "On the other hand . . . "

"Yeah, what?" Tragg asked eagerly.

"Might be one way we can ease your routine some," offered Larry. "It ain't much, but it'd help."

"I'm in no shape for refusin' favors," muttered Dorgan. "What've you got in mind?"

"I'll be nosin' around, tryin' to find some way of clearin' our old buddy in there," said Larry, jerking a thumb. "That's a chore I can handle alone. And guardin' the Queel Hotel, well now, maybe we can take that chore off your hands. We need a place to bunk. Any spare keys to the place?" Dorgan nodded warily. "So here's how it goes. We bunk in the hotel. Night-time, one of us'll be there. We take turns to sleep anyway. That means *we'll* be discouragin' the snoopers and deadbeats right up until the new owner arrives. It ain't much, Jerry, but it'll be one thing less for you to fret about."

"What d'you think?" Tragg asked.

"Well," mused Dorgan. "It'll make night patrols a mite easier. Only I'd have to talk it over with young Marcus. Tell you what, Sam, you go talk to him rightaway and . . . "

"Out of town," countered Larry. "The young lawyer-feller. We met him at the Billings Barn."

"All right, I'll talk to him when he gets back," said Dorgan. "If it's okay by him, it's okay by me. Like you say, it's not much, but it'll help."

"Somethin' else we'll do," decided Larry. "While we're there, we might's well make ourselves useful. Place could likely use a little swabbin' and sweepin'. We'll kind of tidy up over there."

"So them folks from Iowa'll find it clean and shiny," nodded Stretch. "They'd appreciate that, huh? I mean it'd be kind of rough on such respectable folks, travelin' all the way from Iowa and findin' a mess, trash all over the place."

The lawmen frowned at each other.

"I'm tryin' real hard," said the bemused Dorgan, "tryin' to imagine Larry Valentine with a mop and pail

— Stretch Emerson down on his knees and scrubbin' . . . "

"Look, at first we laughed," admitted Larry. "It sounded funny to us, the idea of a family of respectable folks movin' into the Queel House. Stablehand claims it used to be a bawdy house."

"Barney wasn't all that particular," said Dorgan.

"Well, we kind of admire respectable folks, so we ain't laughin' now," said Larry. "Like to make it easier for 'em if we can. Cluff City's got more no-accounts than you can handle, you said. That means the law-abidin' citizens're kind of outnumbered, right?"

"I wouldn't go that far," said Dorgan. "But you're makin' your point. Another decent family'd be mighty welcome. We need as many of their kind as want to settle here."

"Bueno," grunted Larry. "So we'll get back to you later." The tall men drained their glasses and got to their feet. "Got to go talk to a feller now."

99

They traded cordial nods with the lawmen — a rare experience — quit the law office and began seeking a source of information, namely Ralph Gibb, Esquire, editor of the Gomez County Bulletin.

4

Gin and Retrospect

AGED 45, well-nourished but not overweight, Ralph Gibb considered himself to be in excellent physical condition. He appreciated his good health and intended staying as healthy as possible, which explained his trepidation when confronted by the uncommonly tall strangers. A local had directed the Texans to the office of the local newspaper; the door being open, they had walked right in.

Noting the editor's apprehensive expression, the taller Texan smugly remarked,

"He's spooked."

"I wonder why," Larry said poker-faced.

"Excuse me," frowned Gibb. "I'm naturally concerned for my welfare. You see, you gentlemen strongly resemble a couple of Texas-born outlaw-fighters who frequently do violence to newspapermen. I'm Ralph Gibb, editor of this paper. That's my brother-in-law, Ethan Crombie, setting type. As you can see, we'd have extreme difficulty defending ourselves against men of your stature. And now — I know I'll hate myself for asking — but may I enquire your names?"

"He's Valentine, I'm Emerson," drawled Stretch.

"Godfrey Daniel," fretted Gibb.

"Nope," grunted Stretch. "Valentine and Emerson."

"Stop sweatin', Gibb," Larry gruffly chided. "We don't beat up on scribblers that give us what we want."

"That's encouraging — and it raises another question," sighed Gibb. "What *do* you want?"

"Just talk," shrugged Larry. "A few answers."

"That's all?" Gibb asked cautiously.

"Unless you pull a gun on us, which

don't seem likely," said Larry, "you got nothin' to fear from us."

"Always jumpy," chided Gibb's brother-in-law, from his stool by the type table. "Your trouble is . . . "

"All right, Ethan, back to work," frowned Gibb.

" . . . you've gotten to where you believe all the bull you've been writing about them," Crombie relentlessly continued.

"That's enough, Ethan," said Gibb.

"To be as dangerous as you claim" jibed Crombie, "they'd have to be ten feet tall and built like mountain lions . . . "

"For pity's sake, Ethan . . . " pleaded Gibb.

" . . . with fangs for teeth and claws instead of fingernails," taunted Crombie. "With sulphurous smoke coming out of their ears. And anything they spit at, it catches fire . . . "

"I hate you, Ethan Crombie," groaned Gibb. "I've always hated you."

"Why don't you gents quit joshin'

each other," grinned Stretch, "so my buddy can get on with his questions?"

"Mister Valentine, I'm at your disposal," offered Gibb.

"Read about the Mosser shootin' in your paper," said Larry. "You didn't print a whole lot about it, didn't tell me all I need to know."

Gibb raised his eyebrows.

"You have an interest in the case?"

"This is just between us," warned Larry.

"We wouldn't take kindly to you blabbin' it around," said Stretch.

"We'll be discreet," said Gibb.

"We're acquainted, him and us," said Larry.

"You knew the late Beauregard Mosser?" frowned Gibb.

"We know the live Vince Beaumont," said Larry. "And he's no back-shooter. Some things he'd never do. He's no cardsharp and, in a shootout, he'd never draw bead on a man's back."

"Well," said Gibb, "I covered the main points in my report. A brief report, as I recall, but . . . "

"You were there when it happened?" challenged Larry.

"No, Mister Valentine. Heard the shooting of course. When I reached the alley behind the Siren Saloon, it was all over. Jerry Dorgan was headed downtown with his prisoner and the victim's body was being removed."

"So how'd you find out . . . ?"

"Talked to Fogel, Erwin Fogel. He owns the Siren. From him I learned Mosser and Beaumont clashed over a poker game. Mosser turned sore loser, accused the big winner of cheating and slapped his face. The big winner was Beaumont. He threw Mosser out. Mosser returned to demand satisfaction, warned he'd be waiting in the street. To avoid a shooting affray, Beaumont chose to leave by the rear exit. When Fogel heard the shots he and some of his customers hurried into the back alley to find Mosser down with a bullet in his back and Beaumont with his pistol still smoking. Is that simple enough for you?"

"You're doin' fine so far. What's Beaumont's story?"

"I got that from Jerry Dorgan. Beaumont claims he was shot at by Mosser. He turned to return fire, but missed. Then Mosser panicked and began running. Beaumont claims he fired a second shot high over Mosser's head, also claims a third party must've fired at the same time — aiming for Mosser's back. That seems to be his only defense, and I'm doubtful it will impress Judge Spalding or the jury."

At this point Stretch voiced a question. It was pertinent, so much so that Larry mentally chided himself for not thinking of it earlier.

"This Mosser, was he popular?"

"Another of the sporting gentry," shrugged Gibb. "Didn't seem all that likeable. Well, that's just a personal opinion."

"He had enemies," decided Larry.

"That doesn't sound like a question,

Mister Valentine," the editor remarked. "More a flat statement."

"The way it has to be," insisted Larry.

"So we'll be lookin' for a hombre with a reason for killin' Mosser," guessed Stretch.

"A better reason than Doc had." Larry grimaced in exasperation. "I mean *Duke* Beaumont."

"Beaumont's reason wasn't strong enough?" prodded Gibb.

"Not for him," declared Larry. "Not for shootin' at Mosser's back. You know any enemies Mosser had?" Gibb shook his head. "Anything else you can tell us?"

"About . . . ?" asked Gibb.

"We're strangers here," Larry reminded him. "Suppose you talk about this territory. I don't mean for a couple hours. Scribblers ain't supposed to be long-winded, right? How about you keep it short, just tell us who's who? You could start with the sheriff and his sidekicks, then tell us of the big shots, the kind you call leadin' citizens."

Gibb obliged, summing up the local scene with commendable brevity, much to the relief of his two-man audience. He led off by describing Dorgan and his aides as plodding, overworked incorruptibles. The county jailer, Theodore Haskin, was an enigma intriguing to the newspaperman, British and out of his element, an expatriate who would never, could never, be Americanized. Gibb believed it would take many years for local minehands and cattlemen to tire of their zeal for booze, rowdism and general mayhem. Well to the fore of the reformers, the bluenoses, was the most powerful rancher of all, Big Nick Bolt, owner of Slash B, plenty tough, but a bible-reading, evangelistic puritan fired with the ambition to convert the territory to God-fearing, law-abiding respectability. The apple of Big Nick's eye was Little Nick, his only son; though no teetotaller, Little Nick was admired by some for his habit of imbibing no more than he could carry. As for the Siren Saloon, its owner was maybe a cut above the other saloonowners; to his credit, Erwin Fogel did his best to keep his place of business orderly.

Because Doc's trouble had begun at Fogel's establishment, Larry decided they should pay it a visit.

"Next hombre we talk to," he remarked to his partner, "ought to be a gabby barkeep."

"You mind a suggestion?" asked Gibb, as they rose to leave.

"Try me," invited Larry.

"One of Fogel's percenters could tell you considerably more than any barkeep," Gibb assured him. "I've sometimes sat and listened to her when I've had nothing better to do, and she astounds me."

"Why so?" frowned Stretch.

"Besides being talkative, she has a remarkable memory for details, including names, dates and faces," offered Gibb. "For the price of a shot of gin, you're apt to be entertained with a confusing amount of background information on all manner of locals. I can only conclude she has a keen ear and an uncommonly retentive memory. Don't be surprised if she recalls Doc Schubert had a button missing off his vest on the twenty-second of July three years ago. Seemingly unimportant details — she seems to store them away in a memory box."

"She got a name?" prodded Larry.

"Mattie Knox," said Gibb. "A natural redhead — fire-red. You can't see the freckles for the rice powder."

"Muchas gracias," acknowledged Larry. "You never saw us, never answered no questions."

"We weren't even here," said Stretch.

"You got that?" demanded Larry.

"Don't worry," said Gibb, "I can be a clam when needs be."

Mattie Knox of the fire-red thatch and camouflaged freckles was everything Ralph Gibb had claimed, a thin-faced saloon-girl in green satin gown who, when the tall men descended on her, voiced the routine greeting.

"Howdy, boys. Like to buy a lady a drink?"

They shared a corner table with the thin redhead, plied her with her favorite tipple, drank beer and encouraged her to recall the night of Beau Mosser's untimely end. The encouragement, five dollars slipped to her under the table by Larry, won them an eye-witness account of the dispute that had closed the poker party, Mattie having been entertaining a mine foreman at a nearby table. She waxed wistful, heaving a sigh or two, when describing the handsome gambler insulted by Mosser.

"That Vince Beaumont . . . " She rolled her eyes. "Some fine-lookin' dude. Got style. Got class. Didn't rise up and bust Mosser's Jaw. No rough stuff for him. He just grabbed him and threw him out. Listen, I've seen a lot of troublemakers bounced out of here, but that was so fast, so slick. I swear Beau Mosser's feet never touched the floor."

"And everybody saw it," guessed Larry.

"When it happened, nobody looked elsewhere," she assured him.

"Quite a memory you got, Mattie," grinned Larry. "I'll bet you can name every hombre in here that night."

"Oh, that's easy," she shrugged, and the names were reeled off with aplomb. "Other gents in that poker party were the boss and Gus Blackstone that runs the drygoods store and Phil Stone the feed merchant. Chester was tendin' bar. Harv Miller took over from Denver Danny at the roulette layout and Danny switched to faro. Lucas Peach ran the blackjack game that night. We didn't have a full house, but there were plenty customers like Mister Munday the county treasurer and some of his aldermen friends and there was Mister Ed Chilson that's part-owner of one of them mines in the mountains and one of his hired hands, Milt Wynant I think. Yeah, Milt Wynant. And Mister

Scudder was here with his partner, Mister Pitney. They're mineowners too. There was Orin Stewart the telegrapher — he was here for a while . . . "

And so it went on, talkative Mattie seeming good for another hour of such ear-bending, Stretch bewildered by her verbosity, Larry listening attentively, assessing, memorizing. Fifteen minutes later, she was still in good voice, but digressing from the subject of greatest interest, becoming autobiographical. With all due respect for the early years of Mathilda Jane Knox, Larry decided he had heard enough, or as much as he could absorb at this time, thanked her amiably, stood her another shot of gin and departed with Stretch in tow.

They were emerging from a Mexican cafe after a substantial lunch when they sighted the young lawyer again. Marcus Arne had returned his rented animal to the Billings Barn and was being hailed by the sheriff. The Texans watched Dorgan invite Marcus into

113

a saloon and ruled against following. On a sidewalk bench they relaxed, smoking their after-lunch cigarettes, while Dorgan and his young friend drank beer at Suttor's Bar, partook of the counter-lunch and caught up on talk.

Marcus was disgruntled. Summoned to the Scudder & Pitney Mine by the owners to be retained to represent them in a court action, he had been obliged to reject their demands and straighten them out.

"Can you believe this?" he grouched to the sheriff. "They had the ridiculous idea they could recoup their losses by suing the county. The ignorance of Scudder and his partner is just incredible."

"Thought they had a case, did they?" prodded Dorgan.

"It was their intention to demand damages," said Marcus. "They wanted to claim they were disadvantaged by the failure of the county administration to give adequate protection to mineowners against the gold-thieves. You ever hear anything so crazy? To police the gold diggings, Gomez County would have to recruit a small army."

"Scudder & Pitney outfit's been hit twice," sighed Dorgan. "I guess they're feelin' desperate. And I'm gettin' to understand that feelin'."

"With only two deputies to help you — and one of them off-duty — you can't do more than you're already doing," said Marcus.

"I maybe got one lucky break," confided Dorgan. "Mightn't have to fret about the Queel House. Got an offer, but it's up to you, Marcus, what with you bein' — what do they call it?"

"Executor of the estate of the late . . . " began Marcus.

"Yeah, that," nodded Dorgan. "I understand you met up with a couple tall strangers earlier."

"You mean those Texans at the Billings Barn?"

"That's who. Now how does this strike you?"

Dorgan relayed the Texans' offer. Marcus gave it some thought, then asked,

"Are you vouching for them?"

"Damn right," Dorgan assured him. "They got a reputation, boy. What they start, they finish. Oh, sure, they're plenty reliable."

"Good enough for me," shrugged Marcus. "By all means give them the keys."

And so, without public announcement and unobtrusively, the tall strangers were installing themselves in the empty hotel by mid-afternoon, choosing a room suitable to their simple needs, restoring the kitchen to working order, breaking out mops, pails and brooms and getting busy.

Simultaneously, at the Grand Venture headquarters, Ed Chilson had just about given up on his attempts to calm his partner. Since his failure to break into the Queel Hotel, Greg Javert had been like a caged animal. He paced the cabin he shared with his partner, chain-smoking, edgy, oblivious to Chilson's pleas.

"You were lucky at that," insisted Chilson. "No need to keep on fretting about it, friend. You weren't identified, so the worst that happened was you put one of Dorgan's deputies out of action — and who cares a damn about that?"

"Lucky — is that what you call it?" scowled Javert. "Hell, Ed, if that kid deputy hadn't shown up at that exact moment, he'd never have spotted me! I'd have been inside, beginning my search!"

"And finding nothing," growled Chilson. "I still don't believe it. There's no note."

"Mosser said . . . !"

"Mosser was likkered-up and bragging. And Mosser was a liar anyway. Any time he tied one on, he'd shoot off his mouth. He was a big talker. I ought to know. Many's the time he bent my ear with his wild stories, the big pots he'd won, the women he'd had. Damn it, Greg, he even claimed he was a close friend of Doc Holliday and Bill Hickok. Yet you'd believe he wrote down everything he saw that day, addressed it to Dorgan . . . ?"

"I daren't disbelieve it! It's my neck, don't you understand? We'll lose everything if that information falls into Dorgan's hands! We'll be paupers when we hang!"

"I can't talk you out of it, huh? You're gonna try again?"

"Tonight," Javert said firmly.

"Well, if you got to get it out of your system," shrugged Chilson. "And I guess your chances'll be better this time, with only one deputy to side Dorgan."

"I'm leaving *nothing* to chance," declared Javert. "Going it alone was a mistake. This time . . . "

"Taking some help along, are you?" nodded Chilson. "Good idea, Greg. Better to post lookouts."

"Curly and Rydell," said Javert. "I

can count on those two."

"When do the new owners arrive to re-open the place?" frowned Chilson.

"I don't know," said Javert, grimacing. "I only know I have to find it while the place is still empty."

"If there's something to be found," retorted Chilson.

By sundown, the Texans had restocked the pantry with provisions enough to keep them eating three days. With the three-oven stove in perfect order and a liberal supply of firewood on hand, who needed to eat out? They shared the cooking chores, contentedly rustling up a steak supper with all the trimmings. And, later, surveying two laden platters, they mutually agreed they were doing themselves proud.

"Beats roastin' jackrabbit over a campfire," enthused Larry.

"Couldn't smell better if it was woman-cooked," bragged Stretch. "Hell, let's not eat such elegant chow in the kitchen, Mister Valentine, suh, what's a dinin' room for?"

"After you, Mister Emerson, suh," grinned Larry.

With the dining room to themselves, they attacked their supper with gusto and decided congratulations were in order. In just a few hours, it seemed they had accomplished a great deal.

"Old place is lookin' plumb neat," remarked Stretch. "Only a dozen rooms still need cleanin' out. Come noon manana, we could open for business."

"It'll be the Queels open for business," Larry reminded him. "We're just caretakers till they get here."

"And nobody fazin' us," drawled Stretch. "No snoopers, no hard cases, no fool tryin' to bust in for a free roost."

"Not yet," countered Larry. "But it could happen."

"We should fret," shrugged Stretch. "Let 'em try."

"When I sleep, you stay sharp," said Larry. "When you sleep, I take my turn at caretakin'. Easy routine. Nothin' to it. I won't get drowsy till around midnight, so I'll take the first watch."

"Figured you'd want it that way," Stretch mumbled while munching. "Busy 'tween your ears, huh? Studyin' on how Doc got himself in this mess?"

"Got to be a reason for everything," declared Larry. "No way Doc'd back-shoot a sore loser nor any other hombre, but *somebody* wanted Mosser down and dead, that's for sure."

"Some polecat that's laughin' fit to bust," mused Stretch. "On account of it ought to be *him* in that calaboose, not Doc."

"That always boils my blood," Larry said reflectively.

"Uh huh," grunted Stretch. "It always does."

"Wrong man in jail," grouched Larry. "Real killer free and laughin'."

"We've seen it happen often," Stretch recalled.

"Too often," nodded Larry. "Our high-toned buddy ain't frettin'. Can't wait for his day in court, hankers to smart-talk the judge and make Dorgan look like a jackass."

"Ain't that just like Doc?" Stretch grinned sentimentally. "That'll be his idea of a barrel of fun."

"The hell of it is he could smart-talk himself right onto a gallows," fretted Larry. "So, before the judge arrives, I got a chore."

"Meanwhile, we got us a snug roost with all the comforts," Stretch consoled him.

An hour after the taller Texan called it a day, a persistent rapping drew Larry down from the second floor gallery to the rear door. He unlocked and opened up to be confronted by a leering, bewhiskered man in overalls asking for Lulu.

"No Lulu here," he replied. "Place is empty and closed."

"*You're* here," argued the man in need of Lulu.

"Damned if you ain't right," Larry agreed. "But Lulu ain't. Nice talkin' to you — and so-long."

"How do I know Lulu ain't here?"

"I just told you."

"You could be lyin'."

"And you could be beggin' for a faceful of knuckles."

"Think so, do you? Take this!"

Larry took nothing. The big fist missed his head by a full six inches and, in no mood for further boring repartee, he retaliated with a roundhouse right that removed the caller from the threshold. When the bearded man stopped reeling, he came up hard against the brick wall of the building on the other side of the alley. Wincing, clamping left hand to aching head, he made a threatening move forward. Larry dropped hand to gun-butt, showed his teeth and growled ferociously and that did it for Lulu's admirer, who turned and trudged away.

At 10 p.m., two more ex-visitors to the Queel Hotel disrupted Larry's deliberations. This time, he had to open the street door and inform two booze-fired minehands that Belle and Sadie didn't live here any more. To his exasperation, this statement was rejected.

"This's where Belle always is," growled the first man.

"Sadie too," insisted his companion.

"Used to be," corrected Larry. "Not any more. It's a regular hotel now. Well, that's what it'll be when the new owner gets here. Meanwhile, the place is closed down."

"I don't like this jasper's face," the first man complained to his friend.

"Shifty," his friend nodded vehemently and hiccupped. "You can tell from his shifty eyes he's holdin' out on us."

"Stand aside, tall boy," ordered the first man. "We're comin' in to find Belle and Sadie."

"You ain't comin' in," countered Larry.

"Who's gonna stop us?" challenged the second man.

"Aw, hell," sighed Larry.

Around 11.55 p.m., when Sam Tragg

rendezvoused with his boss in front of an assay office, ready to relieve him and begin the graveyard shift, he was moved to comment,

"You're lookin' plenty cheerful, Jerry."

"Wish you could've seen what I saw a couple hours ago," grinned Dorgan. "It's all true, Sam, everything we've heard about those trouble-shooters. We can stop worryin' about old Barney's place."

"On the job, are they?" asked Tragg.

"I couldn't tell if it was Valentine or Emerson," said Dorgan. "Not from where I was when it happened. There were these two big slobs, miners I think, tried to force their way into the hotel. Then one of 'em was suddenly flat on his face in the middle of Main Street and the other one was hung over the hitch-rail. I swear he just dangled there. Both of 'em out cold. Didn't come to their senses till I dragged 'em to the well outside Tolmeyer's store and wet 'em down."

"You're right," chuckled Tragg. "We

don't have to worry about the Queel Hotel no more. Old place is guarded good."

A few minutes after midnight, Stretch appeared on the east side of the second floor gallery, interrupting his partner's prowling, jerking a thumb.

"Your turn for some shut-eye, runt. Town's quiet, huh?"

"Looks quiet now," mused Larry, pensively scanning Main Street. "Damn near peaceful. I've been thinkin' of Doc."

"Uh huh. I'm thinkin' of him too, thinkin' he's likely sleepin' deep right now." Stretch yawned and glanced toward the county jail. "Funny, huh? He ain't frettin' at all, I bet."

"Why should *he* fret?" grouched Larry. "*I'm* doin' his frettin' *for* him."

"Better hit the feathers," urged Stretch.

"On my way," nodded Larry. "Stay loose."

"You know it," said Stretch.

126

It was long after midnight when Stretch, after prowling the ground floor, made his way to the second floor's rear gallery and sagged into a chair, but not to close his eyes, not to relax his vigilance.

The marauders approached very quietly indeed, but might as well have announced themselves by beating a drum or howling at the Colorado moon. Quitting his chair, he crept to the gallery rail, glanced downward and spotted the three dim figures below the firestairs. One of them stayed by the first step. The other two began climbing while, unhurriedly, Stretch moved to intercept them.

Down below, Curly, the lookout, warily scanned the back alley. Not a soul in sight. Javert and Rydell, climbing to the gallery, almost finished their ascent. They were three steps away when Stretch loomed above them, shocking Javert to a halt, startling Rydell.

"Far enough, boys," growled Stretch.

"Turn right round and scat."

Rydell loosed an oath and made the serious error of groping at his holster, but there was no way his gunhand could move faster than Stretch's left foot. His Colt was half-clear of leather when the taller Texan's swinging kick discouraged him. The toe of Stretch's boot caught him cleanly on the point of the chin, and with devastating impact. He crashed against Javert, knocking him off balance. Entangled, they tumbled down the stairs to collide with Curly. Javert's head slammed against a stair post. He went down heavily and was seized by Curly. Unable to move, he was then hauled upright with his arms draped about his companions' shoulders, and then the three were disappearing into the gloom, Rydell bloody-mouthed and irate.

Stretch rolled and lit a cigarette and kept his ears cocked. After a few minutes, he heard the receding thud of hooves and concluded the marauders were in retreat. He was grinning wryly, touching a match to his cigarette when his partner joined him garbed in nought but his Long Johns and hefting his Colt.

"Trouble?"

"It didn't last long," drawled Stretch. "Three this time."

"Old place draws 'em like flies to molasses," yawned Larry. "Every hotpants womanizer in this man's town. They give you an argument?"

"One of 'em made to pull a gun," shrugged Stretch. "I scored on him with my boot. They went down them stairs faster'n they came up."

"Get a good look at 'em?"

"Nope. Too dark. Go back to sleep, runt. I'll rouse you for breakfast."

"Yeah, okay. 'Be seein' you."

Larry returned to his bed and Stretch to his guard duty. From then until sun-up, there were no more intruders. The only other man spotted by Stretch was the patrolling Deputy Tragg, who paused below the northside gallery, but only long enough to trade a few friendly words before moving on.

Back at the Grand Venture in the pre-dawn hour, Chilson waxed wrathful that three cohorts, including his partner, had come close to ending up in the county jail. He berated the sore and simmering Rydell, minus a front tooth and suffering an aching jaw, for attempting to draw on the challenger,

"If you'd had more time to trigger, the shot would've alerted the whole block. You could've had Dorgan and Tragg on your back. And look at Greg. Look at the shape he's in."

Javert was dazed and incoherent. They had removed his boots and deposited him in his bunk, and now Curly was swabbing his head and muttering a warning.

"He could be hurt bad."

"Just concussion I'd say," frowned Chilson.

"Might need doctorin'," suggested Curly.

"The hell with that," scowled Chilson.

"Call a doctor out here and maybe he'll notice Rydell's face. By noon the whole town would know of Greg's head-wound. That'd be more than enough to arouse the sheriff's curiosity. Forget it, Curly. Just bandage Greg's head. He'll come to his senses soon enough."

Javert was still in a groggy condition, but young Deputy Berry back on his feet and available for duty noon of the day the westbound stage brought the Queel family to Cluff City. The ex-schoolteacher had wired Marcus Arne the date of arrival and the lawyer, well-groomed and eager to welcome a better class of potential citizen, presented himself at the stage depot ten minutes before noon. Also on hand were Deacon Dexter Pickard and his matronly spouse, at Marcus's request.

"They're refined folk, Deacon, and will feel more inclined to settle here if they're met by the right people," Marcus pointed out.

The only lawman in the welcome

committee was Ben Berry, his boss and the other deputy being otherwise engaged. But another local not much older than Ben just happened to be in town today, just happened to be in the region of the stage depot when the westbound rolled in and the Queels began alighting. He was the son of the county's reform-minded rancher, a stringy, passably good-looking young feller known throughout the territory as Little Nick Bolt, though he stood two and a half inches taller than his sire.

When Ruth Queel descended from the coach, Nick filled his eyes with her, swallowed a lump in his throat and almost fell off his horse. He managed to dismount and tie his animal without coming to grief, and then he was hustling across Main to join the welcome committee and introduce himself.

Just as smitten was Ben, who couldn't take his eyes off the smiling, demurely gowned Prudence. And, when Marcus doffed his hat to the eldest sister, he was dry-mouthed and well aware his pulse was racing. The depot-boss and the Pickards were shaking Marvin's hand, but with all their attention fixed on Flora and her captivating daughters. When the baggage was passed down from the coach roof, Nick and Ben almost came to blows, each eager to show off his muscle-power by grabbing more bags than he could carry. There was some confusion but, eventually, the newcomers were being ushered into the lobby of what used to be the most disreputable hotel in town.

The Queels had arrived, and now Marcus, Ben and Nick were hoping against hope they would react favorably.

5

Here to Stay

A GREAT many inquisitive locals had tagged the Queels and their escorts to the hotel. One of these, the sore-jawed Cal Rydell, now decided he should cut short his visit and make a fast return to the Sierra Rojo to warn his leaders the hotel was no longer empty. He stayed only long enough to buy a couple of bottles of whiskey before remounting and riding out.

By the time the Texans descended to the lobby to be introduced, Flora and her daughters had inspected most of the ground floor and were waxing optimistic. Marcus identified the tall men and explained their presence here. The new owner then shook hands with them, addressing them courteously.

"So we're indebted to you gentlemen for guarding the property against vandals."

"Is that all you've done?" enquired Flora.

The Texans dragged their eyes from the beautiful sisters to trade appraisals with their beautiful mother. They were overawed, but not dumbstruck.

"Well, ma'am," said Larry. "We tried to make ourselves useful, you know?"

"Like to stay busy," mumbled Stretch, "on account of it keeps us out of trouble."

"Then we have you to thank," guessed Flora. She bestowed a warm smile on them and, then and there, won two devoted admirers. "For the condition of the place, I mean. The floors so clean, the rooms so neat, the kitchen in perfect order." She turned to her husband. "This is wonderful, Marvin dear. There's still much to be done, unpacking, getting the girls settled in, but the place is functional already!"

"Surely we're not ready to accept guests," he frowned.

"Perhaps not," she said. "But we could open the dining room tonight, serve supper at reasonable charges and that would be a fine start to our new enterprise, don't you think? Heavens, dear, the girls and I have all afternoon to prepare a menu and a three course meal. You could print a sign and place it out front and, by the time supper is over, we'll be counting our first profits."

"My compliments, Mrs Queel," Marcus said fervently. "I do admire your adaptability. I am, in fact overwhelmed."

"If you're sure you can manage, Flora . . . " began Marvin.

"Easily," she declared.

"So let's do it!" chuckled Angeline. "What do you say, Papa?"

"Never let it be said I'd dampen such enthusiasm," grinned Marvin. "Choose your rooms, girls, and let's get to work."

"Just one thing," interjected Larry.

"Yes, Mister Valentine?" asked Marvin.

"I'm mostly called Larry," he pointed out. "And my buddy here, he's Stretch. Now, if you folks got no objection, we'd admire to stay on. We've been bunkin' in a double upstairs, Number Eleven and we still need a place to stay, so how about we stay where we're at and start payin' right now?"

"I don't see how we can refuse," Marvin remarked to his wife. "Our tall friends are already installed here, so why shouldn't they stay?"

"And such helpful and obliging gentlemen," smiled Flora.

"Anything we can do, you just ask," offered Larry. "One of us'll be around most of the time."

Real cowboys!" giggled Angeline. "And so *tall*!"

"That will do, child," chided Flora. "Choose your room, unpack, change out of your Sunday clothes and we'll all get to work."

She traded knowing glances with her husband as their youngest girl scuttled upstairs. The lawyer, the young deputy and the heir to Slash B were in earnest and audible conversation with Josephine, Prudence and Ruth respectively.

"Are you listening, Marvin?" Flora whispered.

"Attentively," he assured her.

"It's a small practice right now, Miss Josephine, but I have high hopes. As our population increases, with more people needing legal representation . . . "

"How terribly interesting, Mister Arne, to be a lawyer. A noble calling, I'm sure."

"Sure enough, Miss Prudence. Wounded in the line of duty. Left arm and concussion too. But I'm fine now."

"And you were wounded while protecting our new home, Deputy Berry . . . ?"

"I'm Ben to folks around my age, if that doesn't sound too forward."

"Not at all, Ben, and you must call me Prudence — or Prue if you wish."

"I'd be right proud."

"My pa owns the biggest cattle spread in Gomez County, Miss Ruth, and some day it'll all be mine."

"I'm terribly impressed, Mister Bolt."

"And us Bolts, you'll find us at the county chapel Sunday morning — *every* Sunday morning. My folks raised me to live by the good book and act respectful and gentlemanly around ladies."

"That's obvious, Mister Bolt."

Drawing his wife aside, Marvin said in wonderment,

"It begins already. Those young men . . . "

"All reputable, I'm sure," insisted Flora. "Don't be intimated, dear. We just have to assume the pace of life is faster here than at Purdyville — and adjust as best we can."

An hour later, Marvin reminded the Texans of their offer of help and confided a decision.

"You're not teetotal I imagine. Well, neither am I. Even so, I've decided to close the bar here." Their faces fell. "Hear me out, gentlemen. It's not as drastic as it may first seem. I don't doubt Cluff City has ample saloons, so the closing of the bar in this hotel won't really disadvantage anybody."

"Well . . . " shrugged Larry.

"I guess not," Larry grudgingly conceded.

"You've surely realized we intend this to be a quiet and respectable hotel," said Marvin. "That's the kind of people we are, you see. I doubt we'll be hiring staff, at least not yet. And, running the place as a family business, I have to consider the welfare of my dear wife and daughters. So we hope to attract only the better people. Not necessarily the wealthier folk, but certainly the law-abiding element of this community. How could we cope with roughneck minehands and cowboys?"

"You got a point," nodded Larry.

"In due course, I'll have the bar

divided," said Marvin. "That will give us two extra ground floor rooms and make the Queel a twenty-room hotel. Meanwhile, if you think you could carry the piano out of the bar and transfer it to the dining room . . . "

"Music with supper?" frowned Stretch.

"My wife and daughters are musical and sing beautifully," Marvin said proudly. "They'll be missed at the Purdyville Community Chapel Sundays, believe me. It's just a thought and, who knows? We might attract a regular clientele, people who'll prefer the pleasant atmosphere of our dining room, plus a little music, to the noise and clamor of the local restaurants and saloons."

"Hope you're right, Marv," said Larry.

"Okay, runt, who's gonna tote the piano, you or me?" asked Stretch.

"Enough of your showin' off," chided Larry. "We'll both tote it. Let's go."

Mid-afternoon of this day, assigned by her mother to purchase provisions,

Ruth Queel suffered her first experience of the rough and rowdy routine of a cattle and mining town. The family had visited the local cemetery to pay their respects to the late Barney Queel. Prayers had been said for the happy repose of their benefactor, after which the Queels returned to the hotel to get on with their chores.

Young Nick was still in town, in conversation with a townman of his acquaintance outside the office of the Cattlemens Association when his gaze strayed to the vision of loveliness emerging from a grocery store attended by the grocer's youthful son weighed down by her purchases. Ruth and the toter had walked only a short distance toward the hotel before three off-duty minehands, unkempt, bewhiskered and bug-eyed, barred her way. Overcome by the young lady's charms, they made overtures that started her scalp crawling.

"Thank you," she gasped. "But I do not drink whiskey nor socialize with strangers. Kindly stand aside."

It was Nick's big chance and he wasn't about to pass it up. By the time he reached the dark-haired beauty — now flinching from the questing paws of her unwanted admirers — his blood was up. Fired with the urge to win Ruth's favor, he arrived with his fists bunched, his voice raised in stern reprimand.

"I'll thank you men to unhand the lady and get on about your business . . . "

That was as much as he was allowed to say before a bunched fist exploded in his face, bouncing him off the sidewalk and into the street. To the amusement of the approaching Deputy Tragg, he quickly picked himself up and charged to the attack, only to run into another ready first. As well as the beginnings of a magnificent shiner, his heroism had also won him a bloody nose.

Ruth was frozen and open mouthed, the laden youth also, when Tragg joined the group, growled menacingly at the trouble-makers, emptied his holster and struck out with his Colt's barrel. The first womanizer collapsed where he'd been standing, the second reeled off-balance and nose-dived into a water-trough and the third, while aiming a kick at the veteran deputy, took the weight of the pistol on his left temple; he seemed to perform a one-legged leap off the sidewalk before thudding backside-first to the dust and measuring his length.

"Now, missy, don't let this shake you none," the ugly deputy urged Ruth while holstering his gun and lifting his battered Stetson. "See this tin star? Means I ain't no gun-whippin' rowdy. Regular deputy sheriff I am, name of Sam Tragg. Sorry this happened your first day in town, but don't be fearin' it happens *every* day. You'll be one of the Queel ladies? Welcome to Cluff City."

"I'm — most grateful . . . " she breathed.

And then Nick was bravely resuming

the perpendicular and beginning an apology.

"Should've moved faster, Ruth . . . "

"Should've remembered to duck," taunted Tragg.

"I could've taken 'em with one hand tied behind my back," Nick insisted.

"Your poor face!" cried Ruth.

"I got good advice for you, Little Nick," Tragg drawled relentlessly. "Don't never let nobody tie a hand behind your back. Use both hands. You're packin' a gun. Should've used that too. No law against clobberin' a hombre with your gun when you're defendin' a lady."

"You're so brave, Nick," sighed Ruth.

"It was nothing," Nick hastened to assure her. "Nothing at all."

"And *that's* no lie," grinned Tragg.

"Don't you fret on my account, Ruth," begged Nick, mopping at his bloody nose. "I'll look a whole lot better next time you see me. And that'll be tonight. I'll be coming in for supper in my Sunday-best, all slicked up and looking worthy of you."

"Don't forget to wash behind the ears," growled Tragg. "Meanwhile, little lady, I'd best relieve young Hughie of some of them groceries 'fore his arms fall off and walk you back to the hotel."

Around 2.30 that afternoon, Ed Chilson emerged from the cabin he shared with his partner, closed the door and sauntered to the shafthead where Rydell awaited him. The rogue with the missing front tooth was swigging from a bottle.

"You tell him?" he demanded, as Chilson hunkered down to light a cigar.

"I'll tell him when he wakes," said Chilson. "He's sleeping and, this time, it's more like natural sleep. I think he's recovering from concussion. Time enough later to break the news. So they're staying, huh?"

"They moved in," nodded Rydell. "Queel's brother looks like he ought to be sellin' ribbons in a Bon Ton. But his wife and them four gals of theirs . . . "

"Beautiful ladies?" prodded Chilson.

"Beautiful is puttin' it mild," declared Rydell. "The shavetail lawyer, that Arne hombre, was there too. And the Bolt boy . . . "

"Little Nick?"

"Yeah, him. And the kid deputy. All of 'em droolin' over the Queel women. Won't be so easy now, will it?"

"What?"

"I mean, if the tinhorn really did stash a paper for Dorgan to read . . . "

"Don't tell me you believe that?"

"Javert believes it."

"I know what Greg believes, but I still say he's wrong," muttered Chilson. "On the other hand, I've had my bellyful of trying to reason with him. He won't be satisfied till he's searched the room that used to be Mosser's. He won't find it, and then his nerves will settle — at last. It's something he just has to find out for himself."

147

"But we don't mount another raid meanwhile?" asked Rydell.

"Not without Greg along," Chilson said firmly. "If we run into a fight with trigger-happy minehands, he'd be worth three of you."

At this same time, in the county law office, Sheriff Dorgan was being distracted from official paper work. The noon stage that had brought the Queels to Cluff City had also delivered mail, some of it addressed to the sheriff. Dorgan had letters to answer and bulletins to check, but was finding it hard to concentrate. Though the cellblock entrance was closed, the voice of his prisoner was audible. What the hell? Was that Beaumont dude making a speech? Also distracting him was his back-on-the-job junior deputy.

A few moments ago, young Ben had come hustling in with a small bottle obtained from a barber shop. He stood before the mirror over by the wash basin now and, having anointed his unruly thatch with too liberal quantities of pomade, was carefully plying a comb.

Dorgan was caustic.

"You stink," he complained.

"That's no smell you're smelling, boss," countered Ben. "It's a tasteful masculine aroma pleasing to the fair sex, Rube Garney says."

"What would that dumb barber know?" jibed Dorgan. "He's not even a good barber. I don't go to his place anymore. Last time, he cut my ear, consarn him. How much did you pay for that grease?"

"It's not grease. It's 'Pomade Magnetique' all the way from Paris, France. But he only charged me a quarter for it."

"All the way from a back alley drug store in the red-light district of downtown Denver more likely," growled Dorgan.

"Got to look my best for tonight."

"What's so special about tonight? And don't forget you're walkin' the midnight to sun-up patrol."

"I don't forget which shift I'm

working. But I got to eat, don't I? Dining room of the Queel Hotel's gonna open tonight and I'm hoping *she'll* be waiting on tables."

"One of the Queel girls," guessed Dorgan. "Which one?"

"Her name's Prudence," Ben said reverently. "And she's beautiful!"

"They're *all* lookers I'm told," said Dorgan, "includin' their mother."

Exasperated, he watched Ben part his gleaming hair and comb it back. Ben then turned to face him, grinned eagerly and made the mistake of asking,

"How do I look?"

"Like a dumb kid that just got bounced out of a cat-house because he didn't bring any money," sneered Dorgan.

"That's a helluva thing to say," protested Ben.

"You ask, you get told," retorted Dorgan. "Make it easier on yourself, boy. Buy a hot bath at McIntyre's parlor, get that grease out of your hair, show up in your goin' to meetin' clothes and just be yourself. The way I hear it, those Queel girls are quality. What's the young lady gonna think if you start sweatin'? That'll melt the grease and it'll drip into your apple pie."

"You sure know how to discourage a man in love," Ben said aggrievedly.

"Didn't I hear you were thinkin' of courtin' Harriet Trimble, the baker's daughter?" challenged Dorgan.

"Who?" frowned Ben.

"Forget it," sighed Dorgan. And then he glowered at the cellblock door. "What the hell's goin' on in there?"

Out of patience, he got to his feet, opened up and strode into the jailhouse. Half-way along the passage, he jerked to a halt, blinking perplexedly. The turnkey had transferred the table and chair from his private quarters and positioned them in front of the door of the occupied cell. He was seated and rapping on the table with, of all things, a hammer. The prisoner, fully dressed and with thumbs hooked in

151

the armholes of his multi-hued vest, majestically paced his cell while Haskin reprimanded an imaginary assembly.

"Last warning. I'll tolerate no unseemly interruptions. If there are further interjections, I shall order the court cleared. Kindly continue, Mister Beaumont."

"Your Honor is most gracious," Doc smoothly acknowledged. "I reiterate, gentlemen of the jury, that the impulsive and misguided action of Sheriff Dorgan is indicative of his inexcusable ignorance of due legal procedure. You see before you a man arrested on nought but circumstantial evidence, the evidence being my presence at the scene of the shooting and the fact that my pistol had twice been discharged. What of the third part, the actual killer, I ask? What of the man whose shot merged with mine, whose bullet was aimed with murderous accuracy at the decedent? It is preposterous that I, an expert pistolero, stand accused of this crime. This is no idle boast, I assure you. I am ready and willing, gentlemen, to demonstrate my skill with the Colt forty-five, to prove beyond all reasonable doubt that, when I fire high above the head of a fleeing assailant, my aim is true, my eye keen. It would be *impossible* for my bullet to have struck the murder victim . . . !"

"Order in the court!" Haskin used his hammer again, simultaneously addressing Doc. "We can assume there'd be a noisy reaction at this point, Beaumont old chap. Hugo Kingfisher would almost certainly interject. The crowd would rally behind him and . . . "

"Better to give way to Kingfisher I think," frowned Doc. "Give him enough rope, right? His blustering could antagonize the judge, might even irritate the jury?"

"Gad, yes," grinned Haskin. "Excellent strategy, Beaumont. Excellent!"

Only now did they become aware of Dorgan. He announced himself by exclaiming,

"Great sufferin' snakes!"

"You wish to say something?" Doc impatiently challenged.

"Theo, you were always a strange one, different from the rest of us . . . " began Dorgan. He paused to fish out a kerchief, mop his brow and retrieve his composure. Quietly, he asked, "You mind tellin' me what in blazes you think you're doin'?"

"Assisting the defendant, Sheriff," explained the turnkey. "As you know, he'll be conducting his own defense. Has to be prepared — naturally. So we're rehearsing."

"Rehearsing," repeated Dorgan.

"That should be obvious, even to an inferior intellect such as yours," Doc said smugly.

"None of your lip, Beaumont," growled Dorgan. "I never could figure Theo and I got to say you're gettin' to be as peculiar as him. Any fool who'd get the crazy notion he can bamboozle a jury into acquittin' him — and him not a lawyer — deserves what he gets." He frowned at Haskin again. "Rehearsin', huh? All right. Be it on your own heads. But let up on the hollerin' for pity's sake. I got mail to answer."

As he began trudging back to his office, he overheard Haskin's polite suggestion.

"I'd be happy to step down from my role as judge and portray some of the witnesses — if you wish to brush up on cross-examination technique . . ."

"Those witnesses," bragged the accused, "will be putty in my hands."

"There'll never be another trial like it," reflected Dorgan, closing the cellblock door.

At the hotel, the Texans were still helping out and their admiration for Marvin and his womenfolk increasing by the minute. Undoubtedly, these were adaptable people, resourceful, venturesome and not exactly allergic to hard toil. The kitchen was well and truly operational. Marvin had rustled up the necessary material for the painting of a sign which was placed in a front window to advise the citizenry that supper would be available in the dining room from 6.30 p.m. to 9 p.m. nightly. The tireless Queel sisters had applied themselves to a great many chores, dividing their time between cleaning rooms, polishing furniture and helping their mother in the kitchen. When heavy lifting was required, the Texans were on hand. But they did take time to flop on the second floor gallery, smoke and compare reactions.

Stretch was enthusiastic in his praise of the Queels and Larry in complete agreement, except for one small reservation.

"Damn near every time I look over my shoulder — there she is," he complained.

"Meanin' the young'un," grinned Stretch.

"Purty Angeline," frowned Larry. "Her with her sweet-talk and her 'Ain't you the tallest!' and 'My, you're so strong!' and bendin' my ear about how good she can cook and sew and keep house."

"She don't say ain't," corrected Stretch.

"You know what I mean," growled Larry. "What do I need with a seventeen-year-old taggin' me around, makin' eyes at me, sweet-talkin' me?"

"She bent my ear too," Stretch confided. "Wanted to know what we do, if we're ridin' for some spread hereabouts or just passin' through — stuff like that."

"Her folks ought to keep a sharper eye on her," grouched Larry.

"Better face up to it, runt," drawled Stretch. "She's smit. She's took a shine to you. You handsome heartbreaker you."

"How'd you like to get throwed off this gallery?" scowled Larry.

Then he was wincing to the sound of that eager, lilting, now-familiar voice; Angeline was joining them to announce she had delivered a pot and two cups to their room.

"Can't wait to hear your opinion of my coffee," she beamed. "Mother says I make fine coffee. So does Papa."

"Larry's third wife made great coffee, Angie," Stretch told her. "Or was it his fourth wife? I get mixed up, on account of he's all the time hitchin' up with every female gets sweet on him. He's got a Comanche squaw too . . . "

"And a Cheyenne — and a Navajo," declared Larry.

"I was forgettin' about them," frowned Stretch. "How many kids've you sired, runt? I mean, not countin' papooses."

"Oh, pish tush," scoffed Angeline. "I don't believe a word you say." She giggled as she added, "But you both have most wonderful sense of humor."

"All true," Larry said harshly. "And I'm a woman-beater from way back."

"He's just hilarious, I declare, " she remarked to Stretch as she withdrew. "Enjoy your coffee — and don't forget who made it."

"If it wasn't for Doc," muttered Larry.

"Yeah, sure," nodded Stretch. "You got any new ideas?"

"Not yet," said Larry. "Still studyin' on it. Thinkin' of parleyin' with the gin-drinkin' redhead again, but there's time. Circuit-judge ain't due for another week they tell me."

In the late afternoon, the tall men bathed and changed to their cleanest clothing. They were served the finest supper they had ever tasted since they couldn't remember when at 6 p.m. and, a half-hour later, took up their positions on the ground floor porch to guard the street-entrance against unacceptable would-be patrons.

Despite his black eye, Nick Bolt Junior was extremely presentable in his Sunday suit. He was allowed enter, as were Marcus Arne and Deputy Ben Berry, the latter assailing the Texans' nostrils with Eau de Garney's Barber Shop. Marvin had insisted the tall men use their own discretion in the matter of admitting supper guests; having developed a protective attitude toward

159

the Queels, they were determined to do just that.

Deacon Pickard and family were accorded a respectful greeting and invited to enter. The same welcome was accorded Gus Blackstone and spouse, Ralph Gibb of the Bulletin, Erwin Fogel from the Siren Saloon and Dr and Mrs Emil Schubert. At 6.45, the sheriff stepped up to the porch for a few words with the doormen.

"How about this hombre?" Stretch enquired of his partner. "Think he's respectable enough?"

"I'm leery," Larry said poker-faced. "He kind of reminds me of a burnt-out gunslinger I used to know."

"Quit sassin' me," chided Dorgan. "I got a serious question."

"So try askin' it," invited Larry.

"How're they makin' out, these Queels?" Dorgan wanted to know. "How d'you like their chances of turnin' the old place into a decent house?"

"Our hunch is they'll do just fine," declared Larry.

Dorgan moved closer to the entrance and sniffed.

"By golly!"

"Elegant, huh?" grinned Stretch. "Your mouth waterin'?"

"If that chow tastes half as good as it smells . . . " breathed Dorgan. "Listen, I'll be back. Servin' supper till nine, I see. Gives me plenty time to wash up and change my duds. See you later."

Minutes after the sheriff hurried away, a trio of local ranch-hands swaggeringly arrived, only to be blocked by the tall men. They wore four-day old stubbles and, if Texas noses were any judge, shared an aversion to soap and water. Impatiently, they announced they were here to size up the Queel sisters, said to be the most beautiful women seen hereabouts in a month of Sundays.

"You wouldn't like it here, boys," drawled Stretch. "Too fancy for you, too high-falutin'."

"Some other time," urged Larry.

"Who says?" challenged the taller of the three.

"Just me," said Larry.

"Think you and your skinny amigo can hold all three of us back?" growled the tall one.

"Oh, sure, easily," nodded Larry. "Tell you what, boy. How about you try passin' me? That'll save time. Your buddies'll quit on the idea then."

"You're askin' for it!" warned the tall one.

With that, he bunched a fist and aimed a fast punch to Larry's face, but no faster than Larry's left hand came up to close over his wrist, to check the fist two inches from the tip of his nose. He then twisted the arm, forcing his would-be assailant to yelp and turn. The fist was forced up between the shoulder-blades and the seat of the pants grasped by Larry's other hand. One heave and the rejected cowpoke hurtled off the porch to land in the main street dust with a resounding thud.

"I can do that just as slick," Stretch cheerfully assured the other men. "If I have to."

They took the hint, withdrew from the porch, helped their gasping companero to his feet and hustled him away. The process had to be repeated several times in the next forty-five minutes; two more cowhands, four miners and three booze-blind town rowdies were decisively discouraged from entering. And it pleased Larry to note that these expulsions were witnessed by a great many passers-by. He was no show-off but, as he remarked to his partner,

"The more who see these skirt-chasers bounced, the better for the Queel girls. Word travels fast in a town like Cluff. Won't be long before the no-accounts savvy they ain't welcome here."

Around 8.15, when the dining room was packed with diners on their best behaviour, Josephine seated herself at the piano, improvised an introduction and, in her husky contralto, began rendering a popular song of the time, 'Whispering Hope'. Ruth, Prudence and Angeline, while still attending the supper-guests, promptly joined in, harmonizing, and the clatter and jingle of cutlery was suddenly stilled. For the time it took the sisters to sing that well-loved song, the people were entranced. And then, while the last note lingered, Sheriff Dorgan began clapping, leading his fellow-diners in applause that could be heard half-way along that block of Main Street. The sisters smiled and curtsied and went back to work and the ice was well and truly broken. Not only had the Queels arrived; they had won the acceptance and approbation of their new neighbors.

The Texans, lounging by the entrance, were still on the alert for trouble-makers, but took time to trade knowing grins.

"That'll do it," opined Larry.

"And they only got here at noon," Stretch reminded him. "Think of that, runt."

"They don't waste time, these Queels, that's for sure," nodded Larry.

"Open for business already," enthused Stretch. "Makin' a useful buck already — and makin' 'emselves plenty popular."

Mid-morning of the day after the Queel family's successful debut, Greg Javert removed his head-bandage and demanded to be told how long he'd been out of action. His partner promptly answered that question and reported the arrival of the Queel Hotel's new owner. This shook Javert but, to Chilson's approval, he quickly regained his composure and began planning his next move.

6

A Time For Hunches

JAVERT didn't pace. He stood before a mirror, lathered his face and plied his razor with a steady hand, speaking just as steadily.

"Open for business you say?" he prodded.

"I hear tell they're doing quite a supper trade," frowned Chilson. "Don't know if they're renting rooms yet, but I guess it's likely."

"Twice I tried a break-in and twice I ran into trouble," mused Javert. "All right, a smoother approach will get me into Room Thirteen the easy way."

"Just what've you got in mind?" demanded Chilson.

"I'll pack a bag and visit the county seat," said Javert. "I'll be one of the first to check into the Queel Hotel, Ed,

166

and I'll make damn sure I'm assigned Mosser's old room."

"They've probably cleaned it out by now."

"Well, certainly. But Dorgan still hasn't brought a posse out here, which means the paper hasn't been found. Would the Queels inspect the room inch by inch, check for loose wall-boards, look for something pasted inside a closet? Hell, no. They'd just tidy up. *They're* not looking for a paper that could be the death of us, you can count on that."

"You're a whole lot calmer now, Greg. I'm glad to see you pulling yourself together and I agree this way is better. If it's there, you'll find it. Only . . . "

"Only you still don't believe there's such a paper."

"Right. I still say Mosser was running a bluff."

"Ed, I have to be *sure*," declared Javert.

"You've said that before," shrugged Chilson.

A short time later, neatly garbed and well-mounted, Javert left the Grand Venture headquarters and, by way of one of the regular mountain trails, rode out of the Sierra Rojo. It was around 2.45 p.m. when he entered the county seat's main stem. His horse was checked into a stable in the block north of the Queel Hotel, after which he unslung his carpetbag and walked briskly to that building.

In the lobby, he was greeted by the sensitive-featured Marvin from behind the reception desk.

"Welcome to the Queel Hotel, sir. I'm Marvin Queel, the owner and manager, at your service."

"Plenty of vacancies," guessed Javert.

"Oh, yes," smiled Marvin. "I'm sure we can accommodate you. A single room, I presume?"

"Room Thirteen," Javert said firmly. "My lucky number, you know. Proves I'm not superstitious, right?"

"I'm extremely sorry," Marvin apologized. "Number Thirteen is occupied."

"Already?" challenged Javert. "How can that be — if you've only just re-opened the place?" He produced his wallet. "Listen, whoever's in Thirteen, move him to another room. It's worth an extra five per week on your regular rates."

Marvin apologized again.

"I brought my whole family, sir. We have four daughters and, as you'll appreciate, this was an opportunity to give them rooms of their own. Our youngest daughter is, like you, not at all superstitious, and chose Number Thirteen."

"Makes it easier for you to move her out," growled Javert, his nerves fraying again. "Come on now, I've no time to waste. Have the girl move her belongings to another room — and do it now!"

Though of even disposition, Marvin was human after all, and a fond parent. Firmly, he informed the stranger,

169

"I'm in charge here, and I've no intention of disrupting any member of my family, especially when there are so many other rooms available."

"You're supposed to give first preference to your paying guests!" fumed Javert, as Larry entered the lobby from the rear. "What the hell kind of a businessman do you call yourself? I've asked for Room Thirteen and . . . !"

"And now you're no longer asking," chided Marvin. "You're demanding — and I must say I do disapprove your high-handedness. It seems to me you'd be more comfortable at another hotel."

"Damn it, I won't stand for . . . !" flared Javert.

"*Really*, sir!" protested Marvin.

"Trouble, Marv?"

The deep voice so gently enquiring warned Javert he had gone too far, said too much and said it the wrong way. He fought hard against his mounting fury as he glanced to his left to appraise

Larry, who was impassively appraising him.

"The gentleman is about to leave," frowned Marvin.

"Sounds reasonable," drawled Larry. He arrived at the reception counter, propped an elbow on it and nodded affably to Javert. "Kind of lost your head there for a moment, huh? Happens to all of us some time or other. Well now, as long as you're leavin' . . . "

"Of course I'm leaving," muttered Javert, picking up his bag.

He turned and strode out, after which Marvin winced disapprovingly.

"Most unseemly behaviour, Larry. The man's no gentleman. I mean, to lose his temper, and just because Angeline already occupies Room Thirteen. As if I'd turn her out. The very idea."

"He name himself?" asked Larry.

"Well, I was so taken aback, I didn't think to enquire . . . " began Marvin.

"Don't worry about it," said Larry. "Back in a minute."

When he emerged onto the porch, Javert was still visible, hurrying uptown. It struck Larry as convenient that Deputy Ben Berry was also in view, moving along the opposite sidewalk. Ben glanced his way. He crooked a finger. The young deputy assumed an anxious expression and came hustling across to join him.

"Is it Prue?" he demanded, clutching at Larry's arm, staring to the entrance. "She hurt? Doggone it, she put a chair on the table yesterday and climbed up on it to brush the kitchen ceiling — and that's dangerous!"

"Relax, kid, she's fine," grinned Larry. "Look uptown. See the hombre totin' the carpetbag, him in the grey suit?"

"I see him," nodded Ben. "What about him?"

"Can you put a name to him?"

"Well, sure. Everybody knows him. Name of Javert. First name Gregory I think. Yeah, Greg Javert. He's Chilson's partner."

"Chilson?"

"Him and Chilson run the Grand Venture mine. Real high-paying operation. You sure she's okay?"

"I told you she's fine. Thanks, Ben."

Returning to the lobby, Larry climbed to the room he shared with his partner. He had donned his hat, strapped on his Colt and was re-entering the corridor when Stretch came loafing along from the bathroom. At once, the taller Texan noted,

"You got that look in your eye — like you're chasin' a hunch."

"Gettin' to where you read my mind," muttered Larry.

"Where're you headed?" Stretch demanded.

"Siren Saloon," said Larry. "Got a couple ideas. Need to talk to the redhead again."

"You mean you need to listen to her," grinned Stretch.

"Damn right," nodded Larry. "Exactly what I mean. Get back to you later."

Descending to the lobby, he paused

by the desk long enough to roll and light a cigarette and tell Marvin he was stepping out for a while.

Business at Fogel's establishment was not exactly brisk when he arrived. Mattie Knox, he observed, was alone at a table by a front window. He traded waves with her on his way to the bar, where he paid for a tankard of beer and a half-bottle of the redhead's favorite comfort. She flashed him a bright smile as he joined her.

"Howdy, cowboy. Want to buy me a . . . ?"

"Way ahead of you, Mattie," he grinned, pulling the cork and pouring. "Here you go."

After her first mouthful, she announced the arrival of the relatives of the late Barney Queel and relayed the Bulletin editor's prediction that the newcomers would find favor with the civic leaders.

"Didn't take 'em long to get started. A lot of supper trade they're doin', and Mister Fogel says he's just never heard such beautiful singin'. Seems Mrs Queel and her girls're musical, and . . . "

"I know," Larry said patiently. "We're stayin' there, my partner and me. Somethin' else I want to talk about, Mattie."

"I can talk about anything," she bragged. "Anything at all."

"I know that too," he nodded. "And I'm still interested in what happened here the night the sportin' gents tangled."

"Oh, sure," she shrugged. "Beau Mosser and that handsome feller, the one that put a bullet in him." She paused to roll her eyes and heave a sigh. "Did I say handsome? He's *dreamy*, that Beaumont gent. Awful shame they're gonna hang him."

"Try rememberin' it all again," he urged, "startin' with Beaumont bouncin' him out of here."

"What d'you mean try?" she challenged. "I don't have to try. It comes easy to me."

"So let it come easy," said Larry, refilling her glass.

He drank beer and, while she recounted the events leading up to the shooting, gave her his undivided attention. Again he mentally catalogued details. And, when she finished, he still had a question.

"That's some memory you got, honey, but let's see if you can recall somethin' else. Think now. Think back to when the sore loser called Beaumont out . . . "

"That was right after he came back to — demand satisfaction is what he called it."

"Right. Then he moved out again and, about that time, d'you recall anybody else quit the barroom?"

"There was only one feller," Mattie said promptly. "See? I just never forget *anything*."

"What feller?" prodded Larry.

"Feller with Ed Chilson. Half-owner of the Grand Venture mine?"

"This particular jasper was drinkin'

with the mineowner?"

"One of his hired hands I think."

"Name of . . . ?"

"Well, I never forget a name *or* a face. Wynant it was."

"Wynant." Larry repeated the name thoughtfully. "He come back later?" Mattie shook her head. "Uh huh. Well, much obliged, Mattie."

"You are sure an inquisitive feller," she remarked as he drained his tankard and got to his feet.

"So're you," he grinned.

"Got to have *somethin'* to think about," she shrugged. "Girl can get bored, you know? Come by any time, cowboy. I sure admire broad shoulders. You ain't so handsome as that Beaumont gent, but you got great shoulders."

After quitting the saloon, Larry came upon Sam Tragg intently studying certain aids to the female form divine on display in the window of a ladies store.

"What d'you say, Sam?" he asked by

way of greeting. "You shoppin' around for a present for a lady?"

"Not so you'd notice," growled Tragg. "I was born a bachelor and I'll die a bachelor. Tell me somethin', amigo." He jerked a thumb to invite Larry's appraisal of an undergarment. "How can they do it? How can any female *breathe* without bustin' a gut, hogtied in one of them corset contraptions? Torture I call it."

"Damned if I know," chuckled Larry. "Just a way of pullin' 'emselves together, I guess."

They sauntered a short distance. Tragg nudged half of a cold stogie into his mouth. Larry lit it for him and put a question.

"Where'd Mosser bunk?" The ugly deputy eyed him sidelong. "Well, I'm the one can tell you. At old Barney's place. And I ain't about to forget what room neither. Upstairs. Number Thirteen." He grimaced and, to Larry's amusement, shuddered. "Had to check Barney's register once, noticed the thirteen alongside Mosser's name. Well, by Judas, no way you'd ever see *me* in that room, not even if somebody saw Mosser tryin' to hang himself from a rafter. Thirteen. Hell! Devil's own. Worst kind of bad luck."

"Superstitious, huh?" drawled Larry.

"Ain't you?" challenged Tragg. "Ain't *everybody*?"

"Not me," said Larry.

"Bull," scoffed Tragg. "Every mother's son fears black cats crossin' his path and busted mirrors and thirteen and . . ."

"Not me," Larry repeated.

"Listen, I know you trouble-shooters're supposed to be braver'n most," jibed Tragg, "but you're human, ain't you?"

"Ain't courage, Sam," Larry assured him. "You want the truth? I'm too scared to be superstitious."

"Too scared?" prodded Tragg. "C'mon now. That don't make a lick o' sense."

"It's on account of what I saw when I was just a kid back in Texas," recalled

Larry. "There was this citizen — Uncle Dud we called him — backed right off the sidewalk so he wouldn't have to walk under a ladder."

"That was the smart thing for him to do," insisted Tragg.

"Didn't look that way to me," countered Larry. "Uncle Dud backed himself right in front of a wagon and team, got himself trampled bad. He was laid up a whole month before his ribs healed. Helluva thing. Chilled my blood, Sam, and I've never forgotten."

"Some joker you are," grouched Tragg.

"You and Dorgan gettin' anywhere with them gold robberies?" asked Larry.

"Give us time," said Tragg, grimacing. "Ain't a lawman you could name can be in a dozen places at the same time."

"Grand Venture outfit ever been hit?" drawled Larry.

"No, they . . . " Tragg stopped shaking his head. "Wait a minute. Yeah, once. Only that one time.

Chilson reported it to Jerry later. But, that time, the raiders didn't score. Chilson and his partner and their hired hands, they fought 'em off, sent 'em runnin'."

"Tough bunch, Grand Venture," guessed Larry.

"Must be ten of 'em, countin' Chilson and Javert," said Tragg. "They got the right idea, by damn. Only hire men just as handy with a gun as with a pickax or spade. That way, they can defend 'emselves, make a fight of it."

"Chilson give Dorgan a description?"

"Masked he said. Rigged like Mexicans."

"Which don't prove they're Mexicans."

"Hell, no. You suppose *we* ain't thought of that?"

Before Larry left him, Tragg offered the information that his friend Beaumont was in good spirits and all caught up with the preparation of his defense. Also, the dude gambler and that high-toned Theo Haskin had become close friends.

"You still claimin' you and Emerson're friends of his?" the deputy demanded.

"Stone cold truth, Sam," said Larry. "Only he don't know it."

Javert had not retrieved his horse. Upon reaching the livery stable, he had changed his mind about leaving town and moved on to a saloon. There, with a corner table all to himself, he drank bourbon and put his mind to work, reassessing his predicament.

'No direct approach is going to work,' he reflected.

Balked at every turn, he was desperate now, desperate enough to resort to drastic measures. And, when the solution hit him, he did not recoil from it. What could be simpler — and surer? No rain in this region for better than three months. And, being one of Cluff City's oldest hotels, the Queel place was a timber structure. Dry clapboard would burn like tinder. Whether or not the Queels escaped was of little consequence. What mattered was the damning statement secreted by Beau Mosser somewhere in Room Thirteen. Dry timber burns fast — paper even faster. The only positive means of ensuring it would never reach Sheriff Dorgan's hands.

'Three o'clock in the morning,' he decided. 'No volunteer fire-fighters in this town. Three o'clock — there couldn't be a better time. Few people fully awake, confusion, the threat of the fire spreading. It's perfect. There'll be a patroling deputy, just the one deputy to patrol the entire township, so I need only wait till he's far from the scene. Coal-oil will do it. Half-dozen cans should be ample. Douse the outer walls both sides and out back, throw a match and get away from there fast.'

What could go wrong? Plenty, but this didn't occur to Javert. In his present state of mind, obsessed with his need to rid himself of a threat, he was incapable of clear reasoning. To him, the rashly-conceived scheme seemed nothing short of brilliant; he was that desperate.

At the livery stable toward which Javert had been headed, Larry traded howdies with the hostler and casually enquired,

"Mister Javert collect his horse?"

The answer prompted him to retreat to an alleymouth from whence he was able to keep a fair piece of Main Street under observation. An hour was to pass before he again caught sight of Javert, but he waited out that hour in stolid patience and with his eyes alert. Javert, he noted, made three trips from a hardware store to the livery stable, toting two cans each trip. It was time for him to move to another vantage-point, and this he did, positioning himself close enough to the barn to learn Javert had rented a buckboard. Javert himself drove the rig into the alley paralleling Main on its west side and stalled it a short distance from the rear of the Queel Hotel. He then covered the cans with a sheet of canvas, unharnessed the horse and led it back to the barn.

Soon afterward, sprawled on his bed, Larry unhurriedly reported his observations. When he began the account, his partner was squatting on the near edge of the other bed. As the report unfolded, Stretch had to rise and pace; he was wont to do this when perplexed and, right now, he was one mighty perplexed Texan.

"Yeah, all right, I've heard it all," he frowned, tiring of pacing, sagging into a chair. "And now, just so I'll savvy it, how about you tell me what's on your mind?"

"Be glad to, if *I* savvied it," Larry assured him.

"How about a hunch?" wheedled Stretch. "How about a feelin' in your bones?"

"Nothin's for sure," complained Larry. "Until this Javert hombre makes his next wrong move, all I got is guesses. And guesses ain't gonna help Doc."

Stretch made the effort to put his own grey matter into operation.

"One guess is a Grand Venture man put that slug in the tinhorn's back," he suggested. "Meanin' Wynant, him that snuck away right after the tinhorn called Doc out."

"And Javert's partner, Chilson, could've put him up to it," muttered Larry. "But I need to know *why*, damn it."

"Now I'm as curious as you," fretted Stretch. "What's so special about Angie's room. Sure, that's where Mosser used to bunk, but why'd Javert want it?"

"I got a better question and I sure crave the answer," growled Larry. "Why'd Javert want that room so *bad*? I don't forget the look in his eyes. For a moment there, he looked wild enough to clobber Marv. Somethin's chewin' on Javert and, whatever it is, it's got him near loco."

"Somethin' about Angie's room," mused Stretch.

"Thirteen," said Larry. "And how come all that coal-oil?"

"Half-dozen cans," shrugged Stretch. "If Grand Venture's a big outfit, they'd need plenty oil for their lamps."

"He loaded it on a rig, but didn't head back to the high country," Larry reminded him. "The rig — and the coal-oil — are just a little ways along the back alley."

"So what do we do about that," demanded Stretch.

"Not we," said Larry. "Just me."

"That part I don't take kindly to," frowned Stretch. "We do better when we stick together, runt, when you're doin' the figurin' and I'm sidin' you."

"Can't always have it that way," countered Larry. "This is one of those times, amigo. I need for you to stay inside the hotel. If some other hombre's plannin' on bustin' into Number Thirteen, you're the one'll jump him. I got to be outside, staked out and waitin'."

"The hell of it is," grouched Stretch, "you don't know what you're waitin' for."

"Javert's next move — whatever *that* is," Larry said impatiently, rising from his bed. "He's my chore. Yours is guardin' Marv and his women."

"Somethin's cookin', huh?" prodded Stretch.

"You had to say that," sighed Larry. "Had to mention food. Won't be no supper for me tonight. Anybody asks, you tell 'em I'm tendin' a little business. Before it gets dark, I got to find me a stakeout in sight of that damn buckboard. Hell, I could be stuck out there all night."

With that thought in mind, he unfastened his packroll to get at his poncho. He folded it, tucked it under an arm and, as he redonned his Stetson, traded nods with his partner.

"Stay sharp, huh?"

"You too, runt."

"Yeah. You just *know* it."

Quitting the building by way of the rear kitchen door, Larry rolled and lit a cigarette and scanned the immediate area, but failed to sight a conveniently located fuel-heap, a discarded crate, anything to provide concealment. Disgruntled, he dawdled toward the buckboard. The westside alley was almost deserted at this hour, the few locals walking it sparing him no more than a casual glance.

He paused beside the vehicle and made his decision. The plank fence to his left was in need of repair, but nobody had gotten around to hammering a nail or two where they'd do the most good. To clamber through rather than over the fence was no difficult chore. He nudged two planks back into position and settled down in the easternmost part of somebody's rear yard to begin his long vigil.

This night, the Queels again catered to a jam-packed dining room, word of Flora's culinary masterpieces having spread throughout the county seat. Stretch, on duty at the street entrance, was spared the need to expel undesirables; without exception, the patrons were representative of Cluff City's law-abiding element. Little Nick arrived, this time accompanied by his parents and sister on whom Marvin and his womenfolk made the predictably favorable impression. Also on hand were Ben Berry and Marcus Arne, which surprised Stretch not at all. Though rostered for the graveyard shift, the younger deputy was not to be denied another opportunity to partake of the Queel cuisine and trade pleasantries with smiling Prudence.

Ben, with great reluctance, departed around 9.15 to grab a couple of hours of rest before relieving Sam Tragg. He had to drag himself away. Prevailed upon by the patrons, the sisters again entertained them with familiar frontier ballads, including one that brought a lump to the throat of a sentimental southerner six and a half feet tall, 'Back Home in San Antone'.

By 10 p.m., all was quiet. The last patron had gone his way and the new owner and his womenfolk, weary but happy, were eager to call it a day. Thirty minutes later, the hotel was in darkness, the Queels in their beds and Stretch, still fully dressed and wide awake, chain-smoking in a chair by the window of Room Eleven, ears cocked to the night-sounds. One by one, in the hour after midnight, the saloons closed down until, by 1.45 a.m., the only sounds to be heard along Main and the side streets were the steady footsteps of the patroling Deputy Berry.

The young lawman was three blocks away from the Queel Hotel, his mind on the Queel's second born, when the would-be arsonist made his move. Ben had lost track of time. For that matter, so had Larry. But, unlike Prudence Queel's admirer, he was proof against distraction and ready for anything.

With only the fence separating them when Javert reached the buckboard, Larry clearly heard his heavy breathing. The half-owner of the Grand Venture had led two horses along the back alley, one saddled, the other to be hitched to the rig. Alert, but coldly patient, Larry waited. Not till Javert moved away from the rig, making for the side alley north of the hotel and toting two cans, did he change position. He rose to his full height, glanced after the shadowy figure, then pulled planks away and climbed through to the alley.

When he reached the turn-off into the side alley to sight Javert again, his blood boiled. One can was on the ground. While Larry watched, Javert removed the lid of the can in his arms and made to dash its contents against the northside wall.

"Don't even *think* of it!"

The growled challenge triggered a shock reaction. The can dropped and Javert's gun was suddenly out and roaring and Larry lurching from the impact of a bullet tearing his flesh, clenching his teeth against a wave of pain, emptying his holster. He felt the second bullet's hot breath fan his right ear and, at this close range, Javert couldn't be allowed time for a third shot. Larry's Colt boomed, Javert gasped, dropped his weapon, reeled and fell heavily, and then Larry heard the familiar voice calling down to him from the gallery.

"You hit, runt?"

"Got creased." Larry trudged to where Javert lay, snapping orders. "Stay put. Tell Marv and the women it's all over and I'll see 'em at breakfast. Hustle 'em back to their beds."

"How about you?"

"I'll be takin' this hombre to a doc. That's all for now. Talk to you later. Keep the women away from the gallery. We don't want 'em to see this."

Ben Berry had run two and a half blocks as fast as his legs could carry him. He was panting when he entered the alley from the street-end, too winded for speech. Larry wouldn't have had it any other way. He offered a terse explanation and muttered instructions while holstering his Colt and lifting the unconscious Javert.

"Yeah — okay . . . " Ben was

still panting. "Nearest doctor — the Schubert house — Connor Street. I'll — take care of the coal-oil . . . "

Mercifully, the gash torn by Javert's bullet stopped bleeding before Larry toted his human burden up the walk of the medico's residence and onto the front porch. He freed a hand to sound the bell and, in a matter of minutes, Schubert had admitted him and was leading him to his surgery. Tousle-haired, a robe thrown over his nightshirt, Schubert got a lamp working and fumbled to don his spectacles. He didn't need to order the patient placed on the operating table; Larry was already doing that.

"Chest-wound — and bad," was Schubert's first observation. "Bullet's point of entry — dangerously close to the heart." He accepted Larry's help in ridding the mortally wounded man of his upper garments; only then did he notice the blood on Larry's garments. "How serious . . . ?"

"Him first," insisted Larry.

"Well, yes, naturally, but if you're in pain . . . "

"Do what you can for him, Doc. I can patch myself."

"All right, help yourself to anything you need."

The medico, after a closer inspection of the chest-wound, retreated to a glass fronted cabinet to select instruments. His back was turned and Larry removing his poncho and vest, when the man on the table stirred slightly. His eyes opened. His mouth moved and Larry was quickly by his side.

To catch Javert's barely audible last words, he bent an ear to the contorted mouth.

"Wrong man — in — jail. It was — Wynant — killed — Mosser. Didn't know about — letter to sheriff . . . "

The eyes closed. Larry moved clear of the table a moment before Schubert turned from the cabinet and began preparing to extract the bullet.

"This could be his only chance," he muttered.

"If there's a chance, huh?" prodded Larry.

"Right," nodded Schubert. "Depends on how deep I have to probe."

While Schubert operated, Larry filled a bowl, found antiseptic and cottonwool and swabbed congealed blood from the angry gash six inches under his left armpit. He experienced pain and nausea, but then his vision cleared and, with his pulse beat quickening, he applied balm and a pad of gauze. It wasn't entirely by stoicism that he bore with the pain of his wound. It was his feeling of triumph. He could clear Doc Beaumont now, or at least start the process. He had only to swear an affidavit and put his name to it. Fifteen words Javert had whispered before succumbing to oblivion, fifteen words he had clearly heard and was ready to repeat in court. In court? Hell, there might not be a trial, not for Doc anyway. This information would surely prompt decisive action from Dorgan, a fast ride to the Grand Venture, an interrogation of the man called Wynant. By damn, Doc could be out of that cell by sundown of this day.

"I daren't move him." It seemed a long time before Schubert spoke again. By then, Larry was reaching for his torn and blood-stained upper garments. "I've extracted the slug, done everything medically possible, but . . ."

"How's he doin' now?" demanded Larry.

"In a coma," said Schubert. "No guarantee he'll ever come out of it." He produced a stethoscope and frowned across at Larry. "I see you've been busy too. Sure you don't want me to check that wound?"

"I got it cleaned and covered," said Larry. "Don't worry about me. Just keep doin' what you can for him."

"I'm obliged by law to report all gunshot wounds to my friend the sheriff," Schubert pointed out.

"Don't worry about that either," said Larry. "I'll take care of it. Headed straight for Dorgan's office now."

"Can you make it?" frowned Schubert. "You lost blood. You must be weak, unsteady on your feet."

"I'll make it," Larry said determinedly.

"Brandy over there," offered Schubert, pointing.

A few minutes later, Larry was quitting the Schubert house, enjoying the temporary boost of a generous shot of brandy. He walked slowly but steadily to the headquarters of the local law.

7

Valentine's Way

LIGHT showed in the office windows. When Larry appeared in the doorway, Tragg was squatting on the edge of the couch in his underwear, bleary-eyed, but giving the younger deputy an attentive hearing. Obviously Ben had reported the gunfight and was now rounding off with his account of the aftermath.

"Wasn't much oil spilled. I toted those cans along to the buckboard. Six in all. And, if Valentine caught Greg Javert in the act of dousing the walls . . . "

"Valentine sure as hell did," drawled Larry, moving in.

"Well, damn it, that could mean . . . " began Ben.

"You got it, kid," nodded Larry.

"Javert planned on burnin' the hotel?" blinked Tragg. "Why in hell would he . . . ?"

"Talk to you in a little while," promised Larry, crossing to the cellblock door. "Got to talk to your prisoner first."

"What for?" demanded Tragg.

"Trust me," urged Larry. "Just let me in there."

"Do it, Ben," sighed Tragg.

Larry was allowed to go alone into the jailhouse. Moments later he was wishing he hadn't and feeling angry enough to heap abuse on the caustic dandy. Doc didn't appreciate this intrusion on his repose. From the doorway of his private quarters, the English turnkey frowned perplexedly at prisoner and nocturnal visitor.

"Doc, I've got it all figured out. I can get you out of this fix."

That was as much as Larry was allowed to say before Doc quit his bunk in high dudgeon and denounced him as an interfering busybody and an inept altruist.

"A pox on your meddling, Valentine! I don't care a damn *what* you think you know! Did I not make it clear I'll tolerate no interference? I don't *need* your help, confound you! I and I alone will force the judge and jury — in my own spellbinding way — to acknowledge my innocence! The jury will never retire! Overawed by the unchallengeable logic of my preliminary address, Judge Spalding will throw the case out of court! Try to get it through your thick head, Valentine! Any evidence offered by you would be more hindrance than help! You could foul up the whole proceedings, jeopardize my brilliantly prepared defense!"

Larry made one last effort.

"Better think twice. You need all the help you can get."

"Not from the likes of you," Doc retorted derisively. "Not from a bungling saddletramp of your calibre. Get out, Valentine, and stop poking your nose into my affairs. Out!"

Suddenly impassive, Larry shrugged in mock defeat.

"Have it your way. It's your neck."

With mixed feelings, he turned to walk back to the office. He resented Doc's scathing rejection of his offer of help, but was also grimly amused, confident the imperious dude would end up eating crow, a dish distasteful to him. By the time he rejoined the deputies, he had come to a decision.

Tragg hadn't gotten around to donning his pants, but waxed official nevertheless.

"Jerry's gonna need a full statement," he insisted. "I've heard Ben's side of it, but now we need yours. You tell it. Ben'll put it to paper." He thought to add an enquiry, as Larry helped himself to coffee and perched on the edge of the sheriff's desk. Ben was planted in Dorgan's chair, pen poised over a pad. "How about your wound? You hurtin'?"

"Man gets a bullet-crease, he always

feels it," Larry replied with a tired grin. "You didn't know that?"

"Start talkin'," urged Tragg.

"All right, here's how it goes," said Larry. "I was staked out, waitin' for Javert to show . . . "

"Back up a mite," frowned Tragg. "Leery of Javert, were you? So you had to have a reason?"

"He came by the hotel to check in."

"So?"

"He was cussin' Marv Queel, startin' to throw his weight around, when I bought in and ordered him out. Seems he was dead set on rentin' a room that wasn't vacant. One of Marv's girls bunks in that room. He wanted Marv to move her out."

"What room?"

"I forget. But I don't forget how he tried to lean on Marv. So I got curious, kept an eye on him. And damned if he didn't stash a half-dozen cans of coal-oil in the back alley."

"So you staked out. Just curious,

huh? You gettin' all this, Ben?"

"Getting it, Sam," mumbled Ben, busy writing.

"A while ago, when Javert showed up again and took a couple cans from his stash, I tagged him to the north side of the hotel. He was about to empty one against the hotel wall when I braced him. Then he went haywire, pulled a gun and got off two shots at me, so I just naturally had to defend myself. And that's all of it, Sam."

"Javert's dead," said Tragg.

"Doc Schubert came by to tell us while you were visiting your friend," offered Ben. "Said Javert never regained consciousness, died in a coma."

"What're you gonna do now?" asked Larry.

"No use rousin' Jerry," decided Tragg. "We'll tell him when he checks into the office, or maybe I'll join him for breakfast. Next move'll be up to him. And *your* next move is to sign that statement, get on back to the hotel and flop. You're lookin' toilworn, Valentine."

"I've felt a whole lot more chipper than I feel right now," Larry admitted, as he put his signature to the statement.

When he returned to Room Eleven and began undressing, his partner studied him intently, but refrained from questioning him.

"You're beat," he observed. "It can wait till breakfast-time, huh?"

"That'll be time enough," yawned Larry. "How about the Queels?"

"They were fazed some," reported Stretch. "But I finally talked 'em into goin' back to bed." With a bantering grin, he recalled, "Angie took on till her momma hushed her. 'My poor Larry,' she wailed. That give you a warm feelin' inside, ol' buddy?"

"A pain in my gut," scowled Larry.

He had no secrets from his partner, a loyal sidekick who, when necessary, could be relied upon to stay close-mouthed. Over breakfast, taking that meal out of earshot of the Queels, Stretch listened to Larry's account of all that had transpired, including those few words from the dying Javert heard only by him. Larry followed that with a terse report of his one-sided parley with their mutual friend.

At once, Stretch nodded knowingly and assumed,

"It's gonna be our secret."

"He's got it comin'," insisted Larry, munching on bacon. "Was that any way to talk to a friend? We'll get Doc off the hook sure enough, but I'll decide when and how."

"As for the hombre you had to gun down, *he* sure had a burr in his hide," mused Stretch. "All set to burn this old place."

"Had oil enough to soak the walls all around," Larry said grimly. "If I hadn't been leery of him, he'd have finished it, and you and me would've been all caught up in gettin' Marv and his women out. Whole place is timber and plenty dry."

"She'd have burned fast," opined Stretch. "And why'd he want to . . . ?"

"Our luck's changin'," said Larry. "I already got one answer. Mightn't be long before another hunch pays off. Meantime, we wait and watch."

A few minutes before 10 that morning, while they were lazing in caneback chairs on the street porch, Sheriff Dorgan came into view, mounted and looking ready to quit town. He reined up by the hotel hitch-rail, but did not dismount. His slow nod was all it took to draw them off the porch. Standing by his horse, they eyed him enquiringly.

"On my way to the high country," he confided. "Got to be a reason for what Javert tried to do. Might be his partner knows somethin'. Still and all, the law's the law. Ed Chilson mightn't know anything at all and, if that's gonna be his story, I can't call him a liar."

"I reckon not," agreed Larry.

"Up to Chilson to make the funeral arrangements anyway," remarked Dorgan. "He has to be told about his partner, so that's gonna be my chore. Your wound troublin' you, Valentine?"

"Feelin' a mite easier," shrugged Larry.

"Trial's gonna be set for day after tomorrow," offered Dorgan.

"That soon?" prodded Stretch. "We thought our ol' buddy had more time."

"Got a wire from Judge Spalding an hour ago," said Dorgan. "It'll be earlier than I figured, sure. Seems he's side-trackin' to Cluff, short-cuttin' his way to Denver, got to attend a weddin'. Makes no difference to Hugo Kingfisher. Prosecution case is good and ready, he tells me. And your friend Beaumont ain't complainin', ain't pleadin' for extra time. I swear he can't wait for his day in court, that sassy dude." He grimaced irascibly. "It'll go rougher for him if he tangles with Elisha Spalding. One thing about that judge. He don't take kindly to back-talk."

He raised a hand in farewell and nudged his mount to movement, leaving

208

the Texans to trade glances and comments.

"I like Doc a lot, but I got to say he ain't the most reasonable hombre I ever ran into," Stretch said uneasily.

"That's puttin' it mild," drawled Larry, as they returned to the porch.

"And, if he gets to smart-talkin' the judge . . . " fretted Stretch.

"I'll likely give him time to do that," Larry said with relish. "Let him palaver himself into a corner — before I throw in my ten cents worth. He'll be sore as a boil, and I wouldn't have it any other way."

"He's gonna end up plumb embarrassed," predicted Stretch.

"It couldn't happen to a nicer feller," grinned Larry.

In the mid-afternoon, when the county sheriff reached the Grand Venture headquarters, Chilson's crew of hard cases were performing as busy minehands, doing exactly as should be expected of them; it didn't occur to Dorgan that he had been sighted and recognized while still ninety yards from his destination.

Chilson appeared in the doorway of his cabin, smiling affably and calling an invitation.

"Good to see you, Sheriff Dorgan. Unexpected pleasure. Curly, take care of the sheriff's horse."

Joining Chilson in the cabin, Dorgan accepted a chair, but shook his head in response to the mineowner's offer of a drink.

"Some other time. I'm on duty."

"This is law business?" frowned Chilson, lighting a cigar. "Well now, just what's the problem? If I can help in any way . . . "

"You got any idea why your partner came to the county seat yesterday?" asked Dorgan.

"I talked him into taking a break, thought the change would be good for him," said Chilson. "He hasn't been himself lately."

"Like that, huh?" prodded Dorgan. "Well, I'm the bearer of bad news.

Javert was shot early this morning, died a little while afterward."

Chilson's jaw sagged.

"Hell's bells!" he gasped. "That — that's terrible! A great shock to me and — and tragic . . . " He got to his feet. "You mind if I . . . ?"

"Go ahead," urged Dorgan. "You look like you could use it."

Chilson found bottle and glass, poured and downed a couple of mouthfuls and, with his mind turning over fast, played his role of grieving friend to the hilt. "Poor Greg — more than just my partner, you know. A valued friend. You have the killer in custody of course."

"There'll be no murder charge," said Dorgan, shaking his head. "It's known Javert was first to draw. He got off two shots at the other man, wounded him, gave him no option but to defend himself. And the circumstances were damn strange, Mister Chilson. As well as breakin' the bad news, I have to ask you about your partner, the way he's been actin' lately, anything you can tell me about . . . "

"Strange circumstances?" challenged Chilson.

"Earlier, he was ordered out of the Queel Hotel," said Dorgan. "You've maybe heard it's under new management now, and Mister Marvin Queel aims to run it as a respectable house."

"I heard," nodded Chilson.

"Some time before dawn, he was about to set fire to the Queel place," declared Dorgan. "That much is for sure, Mister Chilson. He'd bought a half-dozen cans of coal-oil yesterday afternoon and was about to empty one of those cans at an outside wall when this other jasper spotted him. That's when he went haywire and started shootin'."

"This is . . . " Chilson shook his head in agitation, "the most incredible . . . "

"It all happened just like I'm tellin' it," Dorgan assured him.

"Only one explanation," said Chilson.

He drained his glass, returned to his chair and sighed heavily. "Yes, that *must* be it. The strain was too much for him. His mind snapped and — he just wasn't responsible for his actions. Damn it, Sheriff, if only I could have persuaded him to consult a physician . . . "

"Strain?" interjected Dorgan.

"Don't ask me the reason," shrugged Chilson. "He wouldn't confide in me. I suppose — I've been half-expecting he'd crack. He'd been behaving erratically for some weeks, you see."

"You want to make that plainer?" frowned Dorgan.

"We fought off a raid, as you know," muttered Chilson. "That was a triumph for the Grand Venture, our men defending us so valiantly, sending those thieves running. I felt pretty good about it, as you can imagine. But, soon afterward, Greg began brooding. We were lucky that time, he said. It could happen again. We could lose everything. That's when he became moody, easily irritated, unnerved. He was haunted by the fear of bankruptcy, of that I'm certain." He hesitated a moment. "I suppose I can tell you this now. It can't hurt poor Greg."

"Tell me what?" demanded Dorgan.

"Just a couple of days ago, he wandered off by himself," said Chilton. "I was worried about him, so I followed him." He gestured eastward. "All the way to the brink of a steep cliff."

"Holy Moses," breathed Dorgan.

"No doubt in my mind now," Chilton said sadly. "I'm sure he was suicidal. He'd have thrown himself off the edge had I not called to him."

"What happened then?" asked Dorgan.

"He dropped to his knees and crawled toward me," said Chilson. "He was raving, Sheriff, trembling, sweating, mumbling incoherently. I brought him back here. He collapsed and, when I revived him — this is the saddest part — he remembered nothing of the incident. His mind was a blank."

"Like that, huh?" Dorgan nodded understandingly. "Well, I guess that explains . . . "

"Yes, a tragic explanation but, of course, we have to accept it," said Chilson. "The action that caused his death was that of a man mentally unhinged, out of control. Lord, Sheriff, this is a sad time for me."

"Want me to set up the funeral?" offered Dorgan.

"If you would," begged Chilson.

"I already talked to Tollard, the undertaker," said Dorgan. "If ten o'clock tomorrow mornin' is all right . . . "

"I'm obliged," said Chilson. "Some of our men will want to pay their last respects. We'll come in a little while before ten. You may tell Tollard I'll take care of all expenses."

In the late afternoon, about an hour before the sheriff returned to Cluff City, Larry warily answered a summons from the youngest Queel. Before following her into her room, he demanded to be told.

"Just what d'you want, Angie?"

"Are you all that nervous?" she teased. "Just because a woman asks you into her room?"

"The word is leery," he retorted, moving in, but pointedly swinging the door wide open, leaving it that way, much to her amusement. "Now what's on your mind? And don't call yourself a woman, kid. Not till you're of age."

"You're fascinating when you're grumpy," chuckled Angeline.

"Don't push it," he warned. "Your pa and me are friends now. If I turned you over my knee, I got a hunch he wouldn't mind at all — but *you* sure would."

"Threats of violence," she good-humoredly complained. "And all because I'm asking your help."

"What's the chore?" he demanded, glancing about.

It was now, he noted, a very feminine room; no mistaking the gender of the present new occupant. As for the occupant herself, she couldn't have looked more feminine, more attractive, in a silk ball gown. Even in grey gingham and a white apron, Angeline cut a fetching figure.

"Nothing you can't handle, even with your wound," she assured him. And then she was solicitous. "Your wound, Larry, is it terribly painful? You've been so brave about it. I think it's just *awful* . . . "

"I've been keepin' count," he growled. "That makes eight times today you've bent my ear about it. Do us both a favor, kid. Forget it?"

"Aren't you supposed to shrug and say 'It's just a scratch' or something like that?" she challenged. He glowered at her. She giggled and raised a hand placatingly. "All right, my brawny hero, it's just this picture."

"What picture?" he frowned, glancing about again.

"This one." She produced the framed print from behind her bed and displayed it for his inspection. "Isn't it lovely? I took it from one of the other rooms. It's called Tower Falls, Yellowstone."

"Mighty purty," he conceded. "But not as purty as that place really is."

"You've been there?" she asked. He nodded. "Oh, Larry, you and your friend are such wanderers — you've been everywhere."

"About the picture," he prodded.

"Well, I much prefer it to that old photograph of General Custer," she murmured, gesturing to the rear wall. "I haven't much sympathy for him. Papa says it's better we feel sorry for the men under his command, all the brave troopers who were massacred."

"Your pa makes sense." He was frowning again. "You want me to take the general down and hang this one for you? Now you know you don't need me for that. You could do it easily, just standin' on a chair."

"My pulse just *races* when you do some small scrvice for me," she said demurely.

With a scowl of exasperation, he moved to the rear wall to detach the framed portrait of the 7th Cavalry's glory-hunter. In doing so, he chanced to drop his gaze to the back of it and note the oblong bulk under the sealing paper. He was feeling at that slightly raised section when Angeline spoke again, this time very softly.

"Larry, there's something I want to tell you."

"Let me have the other picture," he urged. When it was hung to her satisfaction, he tucked the Custer photograph under an arm and started for the doorway. "Don't worry about this. I'll maybe stash it someplace."

"Won't you please listen to what I have to say?" she begged, following him to the doorway. "Please, just this once, be patient with me?"

"Yeah, okay, get it off your — I mean get it said," he frowned.

"I'm not teasing now," she said earnestly. "I'm being serious."

"So there's a first time for everything,"

he countered, but with a grin.

"I know I've been a pest, irritating you all the time, being a hero-worshipper and a nuisance," she said. "But I want you to know you don't have to worry. I'm not really setting my cap for you because I realize there are too many years between us. I *am* much too young for you."

"That's puttin' it mild," he remarked.

"It was only in fun," she declared contritely. "I never met anybody like you in dull old Purdyville, anybody so big and tall and exciting, so I couldn't resist being — well — interested. I'd be crazy to fall in love with you."

"Plain loco," he agreed.

"So don't be edgy any more," she pleaded. "Honestly, Larry, I'd hate for us not to be friends."

"It's a deal, friend," he said with a patient grin.

"All the same, and if you don't mind my saying it, it's a darn shame." For a few moments, she was bitterly complaining. "It's just not *fair*. If I were five years older and if your feet didn't itch so, if you weren't such a wanderer, there'd have been a chance for us. Larry, I've never known a younger man I admired as much as I admire you."

"You will," he assured her. "Give it time, honey. Some likely young feller'll take a shine to you."

"I guess," she shrugged.

"No chance a gal so all-fired purty'll stay single," he said encouragingly. "And you don't have to rush it. Just bide your time, Angie."

"I'll wait," she said. "Women can be patient. We're good at waiting, and that's more than you and Stretch can say for yourselves. I'm right, aren't I? In a week or so, you'll be weary of Cluff City and wanting to take to the trail again."

"You're dead right," he nodded. "Soon as we've tended a little unfinished business, we'll be movin' out. Meanwhile, we don't mind hangin' around, helpin' you Queels settle in."

When he entered the double room, Stretch was on the gallery. The taller Texan didn't stay out there after his partner closed and locked their door and fished out his jack-knife. He came in and, obeying Larry's pantomimed command, closed the window.

"What've you got there, runt?" he drawled, straddling a chair.

"Maybe nothin', maybe somethin'," muttered Larry. He squatted on the edge of his bed, tapping the knife-blade against the photograph's wooden frame. "Might be we're gettin' it all together. Think now."

"You talk and I'll try," offered Stretch.

"We know the tinhorn's room was number Thirteen," said Larry.

"Angie's now," nodded Stretch.

"And we know young Ben got shot at by some hombre tryin' to bust in while this old place was still empty," said Larry.

"Could be the same hombre kept tryin'," Stretch suggested. "He might've been one of the three I spooked."

"So the Queels arrive and what happens soon afterward, like yesterday?" challenged Larry. "A nervy jasper name of Javert from the Grand Venture mine tries to hustle Marv into rentin' him Room Thirteen."

"Marv said nothin' doin' — and then the same Javert tries to burn the place down," frowned Stretch. "So it's for sure somebody's after *somethin'*."

"Angie don't like this picture," drawled Larry. "When I took it off her wall, here's what I found."

"Somethin' stuck under the back," Stretch observed.

"Looks like somebody cut a slit to shove somethin' in, then sealed it with a strip of glued paper," said Larry, plying the point of his blade. In a matter of moments, he was easing an envelope from the backing, discarding the photograph, studying that envelope with keen interest. "Well, now."

"Got writin' on it," remarked Stretch. "What's it say?"

223

"To be opened in the event of my death by the sheriff of Gomez County," growled Larry. "And there's a name on it. Beauregard Mosser."

"Pay-dirt," grinned Stretch. "So what're you waitin' for?"

"Who's waitin'?" shrugged Larry, tearing the flap. "For all we know, this could be too rich for Jerry Dorgan's blood. Be pure christian kindness if we read it first."

"We're the kindliest hombres I ever heard of," Stretch said poker-faced.

There were two sheets. Larry unfolded them and, for several minutes, was absorbed in his reading of the dead gambler's revelations. Stretch, rolling a cigarette, studied his partner's changing expressions, the raising of an eyebrow, the fleeting frowns, the brief, mirthless grins. When Larry returned the statement to the envelope and pocketed it, he lit his cigarette and invited him to share the information.

"I'll settle for just the gizzard of it, runt."

"But for this damn gash," said Larry, wincing and feeling at his wound, "I'd pass it on to Dorgan rightaway."

"You ain't healin' so fast this time?" challenged Stretch.

"A little extra time'll make a heap of difference," opined Larry. "Day after tomorrow, for instance. Right after the trial. Or maybe while we're still in court. When Dorgan moves against the gold-thieves, I'd admire to side him."

"You and me both," insisted Stretch.

"Uh huh," grunted Larry. "Better that way. Till then, we keep it to ourselves."

"And what've we got?" asked Stretch.

"Everything Dorgan needs," said Larry. "Here's how it adds up. Every so often, Mosser'd stash a new deck in his pocket and ride to the gold diggin's for a little action, little poker party with a bunch of prospectors. That's how he spotted the raiders."

"Hey now," breathed Stretch.

"Seven of 'em, still masked and with their loot slung to their horses," said

Larry. "On their way home from a raid, you know? They were killin' their back-trail, travelin' Ramblin' Rattlesnake Creek. They didn't spot him, so he tagged 'em. Along the way, they got rid of the masks. And where d'you suppose they ended up? Grand Venture mine. Chilson, Javert and five others."

The taller Texan grimaced in disgust.

"They've been gettin' rich, but not from sweat and toil. Doin' it the easy way."

"Some greedy sonofagun he was, that Mosser," drawled Larry. "Waited till next time Chilson came to town, then put the arm on him, told Chilson what he saw, warned he'd turn 'em in 'less he got paid to keep his mouth shut. Chilson had to deal him in for a fat share of all the gold they hijacked."

"Good deal for Mosser," remarked Stretch, "till he got to frettin', fearin' he'd end up in an alley with a knife in his back or his head stove in. So he wrote it all down for Jerry Dorgan. But, listen now, if they knew he did that, why'd they take such a chance? You said Javert told you it was Wynant killed Mosser."

"Somethin' else he said," Larry reminded him. "Wynant didn't know about the letter. If I had to make a guess, I'd say Mosser didn't tell all of 'em. Might be Javert was the only one knew. And Javert wasn't in the saloon when Doc locked horns with the tinhorn."

"Sure explains why Javert was crazy to get into Angie's room," muttered Stretch.

"And Mosser had no fear of goin' to prison," said Larry. "What he did, the law calls it blackmail, but he didn't care. He knew, if Dorgan ever read what he wrote, he'd be too dead to care."

"Everything comes to him that waits," Stretch said cheerfully. "We got it all, runt."

"And then some," nodded Larry. "We can give Dorgan the real killer and, for a bonus, steer him to the

Grand Venture bunch."

"But it can wait a couple days," said Stretch.

"Doc's day in court's the right time for it," Larry was adamant.

"Still sore at him, huh?" grinned Stretch.

"I'm no grudge-toter," shrugged Larry.

"The hell you ain't," scoffed Stretch.

"Let's just say the timin's got to be right," suggested Larry.

Late afternoon of the following day, the gaunt, craggy-browed, seemingly ageless Judge Elisha Spalding arrived in Cluff City in the buggy he'd been using for as long as Sheriff Dorgan could remember. Dorgan and the county prosecutor were on hand to greet him and to answer his usual question — how many cases pending? The judge was gratified to learn he was to hear only one case, but not so gratified when told it was to be a murder trial and even less gratified, disgruntled in fact, that the accused intended conducting his own defense.

"Unwise at best," was his reaction. "Time-wasting at worst. Always long-winded these amateurs. Is the defendant a man of some education?"

"Of considerable education," offered Hugo Kingfisher, he of the baggy suit, flabby frame and purple proboscis.

"That'll make it worse still," grouched Spalding. "The more educated they are, the greater the danger they'll resort to high-falutin' rhetoric. I can but cling to the hope it'll be a one-day sitting."

"Got a suggestion for you, Judge," offered Dorgan. "If you want to check into the Montague Hotel just like always, that's up to you, but . . . "

"When you've lived as long as I have, you get to be a creature of habit," sighed Spalding. "The beds at the Montague are lumpy and the cuisine leaves much to be desired, but I guess I'm conditioned to it. On the other hand, if accommodation for transients has improved since I was last in Cluff

City, I'm open to suggestions, Sheriff Dorgan."

"Like to recommend the Queel place," said Dorgan. "Under new management. Pretty much a family-type hotel now. And the food . . . "

He rolled his eyes.

"You're drooling, Sheriff Dorgan," observed the judge. "Like to take care of my horse while Hugo escorts me to the Queel Hotel?"

After a fine supper, a restful night's sleep and a just as appetizing breakfast, the circuit-judge's mood was more genial when he took his place on the bench at 9.30 next morning. Already present were the usual curious locals with nothing better to do, plus a few new faces. The tall Texans were seated well to the fore, having arrived early. Close by and as comely a spectator as had ever been seen in the Gomez County Courthouse was Miss Prudence Queel, her badge-toter admirer having suggested this would be an ideal opportunity for her to observe the skill and aplomb with which he performed the duty of junior court orderly. Sam Tragg was minding the office, which meant Theodore Haskin was able to attend, cutting a dignified figure in his only surviving Saville Row outfit. Volunteers for jury duty were very much in evidence.

Another interested party on hand was Milt Wynant of the Grand Venture mine who, to Chilson's amusement, had insisted he wasn't about to miss this once-in-a-lifetime experience; a scapegoat tried and convicted with the real killer as an observer.

Exactly one minute after Judge Spalding arrived, the county prosecutor heaved his bulk from his chair the better to witness the entrance of the accused and the escorting Sheriff Dorgan. The judge was as interested as Kingfisher.

Also apprehensive.

8

The Thunder-Plunderers

POTENTIAL witnesses, such as Gus Blackstone, did not share the attitude of disapproval shown by Judge Spalding and Hugo Kingfisher. Blackstone and others were overawed by the Beaumont entrance, the Beaumont demeanor and the Beaumont flair. Assured by Doc that handcuffs would be unnecessary, Dorgan had taken him at his word. Now, keeping pace with Doc's stately tread down the centre aisle, Dorgan was regretting having used the main entrance, wishing he had hustled the prisoner in through the side door like any common miscreant.

It was Doc's moment and he was living it to the full. In his custom-made frock coat, striped pants and multi-hued vest, he was the centre of all eyes, advancing purposefully, head held high, well-brushed hat in the crook of his left arm, his two-inch thick sheaf of notes held to his chest.

Overcome, Blackstone rose and clapped. Spalding banged with his gavel while Kingfisher snorted ferociously. To Spalding's further disapproval, Doc paused to acknowledge the tribute, bowing in courtly fashion to the storekeeper.

"If there is the slightest hint of a demonstration here . . . " threatened Spalding.

"Siddown, Gus," growled Dorgan, and Blackstone resumed his seat.

Reaching the front end of the courtroom, Doc bowed again, this time to the judge.

"Vincent Beaumont, Your Honor," he announced. "I appear as both accused and defense counsel. Your Honor and gentlemen of the jury, you see before you an innocent man of noble origin and unblemished character — arrested on circumstantial evidence which can be described as flimsy at best. It is a travesty of justice that I stand accused of the wanton murder of . . . "

"Silence!" gasped Spalding, using his gavel again. "Great balls of fire!"

"Your Honor?" frowned Doc.

"Mister Beaumont," scowled Spalding. "You're off to a less than impressive start, to put it mildly. Certain time-honored procedures are still observed. This will no doubt come as a surprise to you, but it is far too early for you to address the jury — mainly because there is not yet a jury. We have to empanel a jury, you see, and we haven't yet gotten around to that very necessary chore. As a matter of fact . . . " The court was tomb-quiet, but he banged his gavel anyway and turned beetroot-red, "this court isn't even in session!"

"As your Honor pleases," said Doc, bowing again.

"You *bet* my honor pleases!" snapped Spalding. "Sheriff Dorgan, kindly put a tight rein on your prisoner!"

234

"You sit now," Dorgan told Doc. "Right here."

Doc took the seat indicated by Dorgan, after which the usual preliminaries were observed. And then, during the empanelling of jurymen, Larry won Dorgan's attention by the simple expedient of rising, moving into the aisle and backstepping toward the rear of the court. His urgent nod was all it took to prompt Dorgan to follow. At his boss's signal, Ben Berry changed position to stand guard on the accused; he did this in a forthright and square-shouldered way calculated to impress Prudence.

When Dorgan joined him in the lobby, Larry addressed him tersely and without raising his voice. Dorgan also kept his voice low, but it shook a lot as he gaped and complained,

"You had to leave it till *now*? You couldn't tell me earlier?"

"Give me time," soothed Larry. "You'll get used to the way I do things."

"Never in a million years!" gasped Dorgan.

"About this Wynant hombre," prodded Larry. "He here?"

"He's here," nodded Dorgan.

"See how helpful I'm bein'?" challenged Larry. "I'm savin' you time and trouble. This way, you don't have to ride to the high country and . . . "

"You should've told me *rightaway*," protested Dorgan.

"Better late than never," shrugged Larry. "Now here's what you do, Jerry ol' buddy."

He imparted instructions and advice that caused Dorgan's eyes to bulge, then proffered the envelope once secreted behind the frame photograph of George Armstrong Custer, suggesting Dorgan read it while he, a last minute witness, addressed the court.

"I don't know if Judge Spaldin'll allow . . . " began Dorgan.

"He can't hang you for tryin'," Larry said cajolingly.

Dorgan stowed the envelope in his

hip pocket and followed Larry back into the courtroom and down the centre aisle. In the box, a prospective juryman was earnestly boring Spalding out of his mind with a recitation of his fine qualities and capacity for impartiality. Spalding was, in fact, grateful for the interruption.

"Sheriff Dorgan?"

"It's this way, Your Honor," frowned Dorgan. "Certain information has just now come to light. This man — name of Lawrence Valentine — is known to me as — uh — bein' of good character, meanin' he'd never lie to you."

At once, Doc was on his feet and glaring at Larry.

"I object!" he thundered.

"You *what*?" blinked Spalding. He reached for his gavel again and, for a harrowing moment, Dorgan feared he would fling it, aiming for the accused's noble head. "Last warning, Beaumont! Be seated and be quiet — or I'll order the deputy to muzzle you until it comes time for you to make your opening address!"

Doc aimed a desperate glance at Haskin, who shrugged helplessly. In chagrin, he sagged to his chair.

"If Valentine is allowed tell what he knows — with your permission that is," said Dorgan, "these proceedin's could be — well — shortened. I mean — there'd be no need for a jury."

Suddenly, Spalding was impassive as a veteran poker player sitting behind a pat hand. The word 'shortened' was infinitely appealing to him, a lure, a straw to be clutched. His gaze switched to Larry.

"I am tempted," he declared, "to dispense with procedure and permit you to speak at this time. I'd have to insist, however, that you give this information under oath."

"I'm willin', Judge," drawled Larry.

"Take the stand then," ordered Spalding.

The gabby potential juryman was obliged to vacate the box to make way for Larry, who then placed a hand on the bible held by Dorgan and swore to tell the truth, the whole truth and nothing but the truth. Dorgan now retreated to the rear of the court, fished the Mosser statement from his pocket and began reading it.

Larry led off by recounting the circumstances of his gun-duel with the late Gregory Javert. During this, there were no protests from Doc nor the nose-scratching Hugo Kingfisher nor, for that matter, anybody else. A dropped pin would have been distinctly audible when he paused briefly.

"I carried Javert to Doc Shubert's place," he continued. "Javert opened his eyes and his mouth while the doc was checkin' his gear for — I think he called it a probe. I put my ear to Javert's mouth and he talked."

Spalding interrupted for the first time.

"Not for long, surely?"

"Not for long," nodded Larry. "He didn't say much, but I caught it all and

I don't forget any of it, not one word of it."

"His exact words then?" prodded Spalding.

"He said," declared Larry, "wrong man in jail. It was Wynant killed Mosser. Didn't know about letter to sheriff."

"Thunderation," rumbled Kingfisher.

Dorgan was still reading, and intently, when Wynant quit his seat and bumped the knees of locals on his way to the aisle. Stretch, who had turned to keep an eye on the crowd, felt for the butt of his right hand Colt, then grinned indulgently at Ben, on his feet now, filling his hand and leveling his six-shooter at the man now in the aisle and making for the rear of the courtroom.

"Don't take another step, Wynant!" he yelled. "And keep your hand clear of your holster! You're covered!"

The Texans shrugged resignedly and Spalding grimaced in exasperation as scveral females took their cue, loosed ear-piercing screams and swooned. To her credit, Prudence Queel disassociated herself from these standard gestures; she was too busy for hysteria, her rapt gaze on her hero. At the end of the aisle, Dorgan hastily shoved the envelope and papers into his shirt, whipped out his colt and drew a bead on the frozen Wynant. The killer was haggard and wild-eyed now, sweat streaming down his face.

"Raise your paws!" scowled Dorgan. "I'm takin' you in!"

"It's all lies!" cried Wynant.

"Mister Valentine has repeated the last words of a dying man — under oath," growled Spalding. "I call that reason enough for taking you into custody, at least for questioning."

"Deputy Berry, move up behind him, but don't get *right* behing him," ordered Dorgan. "Take his weapon."

As well as disarming the trembling Wynant, Ben manacled his hands behind his back. And now Kingfisher, beside himself with curiosity, rose to insist to the judge,

"This man's statement changes the complexion of the case against the accused, of that there can be no doubt, Your Honor. But it does seem incomplete."

"You have questions, Mister Prosecutor," guessed Spalding.

"Two," said Kingfisher. "How was this wanton murder committed — in such a way as to divert blame to the accused Beaumont? And what of the motive?"

With his junior deputy well and truly in charge of Wynant, Dorgan deemed it safe to hurry down the aisle to confront the judge.

"Beaumont's claim makes sense now, Your Honor," he offered. "He insisted his last shot — fired over Mosser's head — seemed uncommon loud and — uh — seemed to last . . . "

"That's what I mean," nodded Dorgan. "Well now, if Wynant had a bead on a runnin' man from somewhere behind Beaumont, if he triggered at the same time Beaumont . . . "

"It would seem Beaumont was the victim of a dastardly . . . " began Kingfisher.

"He was set up," Larry said flatly.

"But the motive," frowned Kingfisher.

Dorgan took the Mosser statement from his shirt, approached the bench and proffered it.

"Take a couple minutes to read this, Your Honor. It was found — uh — only a little while ago — and I reckon it explains everything. I mean, when you add it to Javert's dyin' words."

Spalding adjusted his spectacles and the tense silence persisted; even the men fanning the swooners, trying to bring them round, worked quietly. Everybody else watched the judge. Slowly, Spalding refolded the papers and restored them to the envelope. As he returned it to Dorgan, he enquired,

"Will it be possible to verify this statement was written by the murder victim?"

"Any samples of Mosser's fist?" demanded Kingfisher.

"There's the hotel register," suggested Dorgan. "And I got somethin' in my files. He was arrested once for mixin' into a fight at the Four Jacks Saloon. I can find the paper he wrote on, listin' the contents of his pockets. And, when I discharged him from custody, I know I made him sign a receipt for his personal effects. That's regular procedure, you know?"

"Let me have a form of warrant as soon as possible," urged Spalding. "I'll authorize you to . . ."

"Better if you don't say it out loud," warned Dorgan. "Beggin' your pardon."

"Your caution is admirable, Sheriff," Spalding said approvingly. "You'll be authorized then to proceed to a certain location and take certain parties into custody." He nodded to Larry. "The court is obliged to you. As you promised, you certainly have shortened these proceedings, and I'm most grateful. Sheriff, you may release the prisoner."

"Damn you, Valentine . . . " raged Doc.

"Take it easy, amigo," grinned Larry, descending from the stand. "All I did was clear you."

To the judge, Doc bitterly complained.

"I am being thwarted in my attempt to prove to this court the incompetence of the Gomez County law authorities! This is an outrageous attack on my rights as a . . . !"

"That will do, sir!" scowled Spalding, rising to glower at him. "In all my years as a circuit judge, you are the first, the only defendant I've heard protest the dismissal of a murder charge. It has been proved to my satisfaction you were the victim of a shabby conspiracy and, had the conspirators not been exposed, I'd have sentenced you to hang for a crime you did not commit. You are exonerated, Beaumont. You are being set free — yet you complain? I warn you . . . " He pointed sternly. "Unless you leave this courtroom now, this very moment, I'll declare you a dangerous lunatic and order you kept in custody pending a medical examination of your head!" He banged his gavel. "This court is adjourned!"

Outside the courthouse, after acknowledging Haskin's short speech of sympathy, the irate dandy sought out the Texans. Haskins followed the lawmen and their prisoner to the county jail; already he had decided it would be poetic justice to install Wynant in the cell previously accommodating Doc.

When Doc finally caught up with the tall men, his innate chivalry demanded he refrain from ungentlemanly abuse; they were escorting Prudence back to the hotel. He choked back his fury and doffed his hat as Larry performed introductions.

"Your servant, Miss Queel," he muttered.

"How gallant, Mister Beaumont," she smiled. "And how grateful you must be for Larry's intervention on your behalf. Now that we're acquainted, sir, it is clear to me you could *never* be a murderer — or any kind of rogue."

"Remember now, Prue honey," drawled Stretch. "When you hear of sportin' gents . . . "

"Meanin' professional gamblers," interjected Larry.

" . . . don't be thinkin' they're all slickered-up dudes, cheaters, cardsharps and the like," Stretch counselled. "Many a gamblin' man, like our friend here, is plumb respectable and a regular gentleman."

"I'm sure that's true," said Prudence.

"Very gracious of you," Doc stiffly acknowledged.

He held himself in check until they reached the hotel. From the bottom of the steps, they watched the dark-haired beauty climb to the porch. She paused in the entrance to smile back at them. Three Stetsons, one black and spotless, two colorless, battered and sweat-stained, were raised. Then Prudence moved into the lobby and

Doc whirled on the tall men.

"For this, I'll never forgive you!" he stormed. "Not content with stealing my thunder, ingratiating yourselves with that muddle-headed judge, you held me up to ridicule! Damn you, Valentine, I warned you against meddling . . . !"

"Things just happened, Doc," drawled Stretch.

"We got lucky is all," shrugged Larry. "We knew the real killer was right there in court, so what else could we do? I was duty-bound to stand by the law and tell what I knew. You want me to apologize for savin' your neck? Okay, I sure beg your pardon." He glanced toward the county jail. "Listen, we'd admire to hang around and chew the fat with you, but we still got unfinished business. Let's get together later, huh?"

"Be seein' you, Doc," grinned Stretch.

The Texans separated, Larry beelining for the Billings barn, Stretch hustling into the hotel. Still seething, about to move on to the law office to demand the return of his bankroll and personal effects, Doc was descended upon by the broad-grinning Erwin Fogel and the elated Gus Blackstone, both warmly congratulating him, pumping his hand, assuring him they had never doubted his innocence. And, when Fogel insisted he accompany them to the Siren to celebrate the clearing of his name, he decided to postpone the repossession of his belongings. His money would be no good at the Siren anyway; he was Fogel's guest.

A short time later, when the tall men appeared in the law office doorway, they were obliged to sidestep to avoid collision with Ben Berry, on his way out and in a hurry, hefting a shotgun. Haskin was in the jailhouse with the new prisoner. Dorgan and Tragg had donned their hats and were loading shotguns.

"Ready when you are, Jerry ol' buddy," Stretch cheerily announced.

Dorgan cold-eyed Larry and muttered a reproach,

"You took your own sweet time tippin' me off."

"No use gettin' sore," frowned Larry. "We're willin' to help . . . "

"Any way *you* see fit," accused Dorgan.

"Our way could save you a mess of trouble," Larry assured him. "And maybe a couple pints of blood."

"Blood?" challenged Dorgan.

"You get hit by a bullet, you bleed," explained Stretch. "You didn't *know* that?"

"Now just a damn minute . . . !" began Dorgan.

"Might's well hear 'em out, Jerry," suggested Tragg. "What can it cost you?"

"It's just an idea," Larry said placatingly. "We'll talk it over on our way to the Grand Venture."

"Best take us along, Jerry," urged Stretch. "Save yourself the time and trouble of deputin' a posse."

The Texans had their way. When Ben returned to the law office mounted and leading two saddled horses, Dorgan and Tragg moved out with the tall men and at once noted the sorrel and pinto waiting at the hitch-rail. Three duly-appointed lawmen and two outlaw-fighters then rode out of Cluff City, bound for the Sierra Rojo.

There was no further conversation until, reaching the foothills, the five called a halt to spell their animals. Larry said his piece briefly, but compellingly.

"This Chilson skunk don't know us. Better we go in first, Jerry. Before you show yourselves I mean. You already told us this is a rough outfit. As well as all the gold they've grabbed, they got some killin' to answer for. So what d'you suppose is gonna happen if we all ride in and they sight three tin stars?"

"He's got a point, Jerry," frowned Tragg. "They'd likely spook and fill their hands. Could be a shoot out. And there's more of 'em than us."

"You and Emerson first?" challenged Dorgan.

"While you stakeout," nodded Larry.

"We'll play it friendly at the start, give Chilson a big howdy and walk right up to him. Then one of us'll put a gun to his head and order him to call his men out with their hands up."

"Now you got to admit," said Stretch, "that makes better sense than chargin' in bull-headed and maybe gettin' blowed out of our saddles."

"I'm not backing down from a fight, Mister Dorgan," muttered Ben. "But I'm for doing it Larry's way."

"I wasn't about to put it to a vote," sighed Dorgan. "All right, Valentine, if we can take 'em without bloodshed, that'll suit me fine."

"Just so we'll know who to jump," Larry thought to enquire, "what kind of lookin' hombre is this Chilson?"

It was around 12.30 p.m. when Dorgan next called a halt. Dead ahead was a bend of the trail winding toward the Grand Venture. It now occurred to him a lookout might be posted and, remembering his last visit to this area, he decided this was as far as they could advance undetected.

"We'll give you a five minute start," he told Larry, "leave our animals here and follow you afoot. That way, we won't be too far behind you."

"Long as you ride slow," cautioned Tragg.

"You got it," nodded Larry.

Unhurriedly, he moved on stirrup-to-stirrup with Stretch. They rounded the bend and continued to dawdle their horses upward, boredly scanning the terrain ahead and to either side, seemingly relaxed, but missing nothing. It was Stretch who sighted the lookout.

"Rifleman," he said casually. "On a high rock about thirty yards ahead and left of us."

"Bueno," grunted Larry.

When he too sighted the guard, he rose in his stirrups, waved to him in friendly fashion, pointed ahead and called a question.

"Grand Venture — this way?"

The rifleman nodded and promptly disappeared. From there to their destination, the Texans sensed he was keeping pace. When he next appeared, he was straddling a black colt and moving along a short distance ahead of them, studying them over his shoulder.

They followed the guard into the area between the cabins and the shaftheads and, sighting picketed horses, nudged their mounts towards them. During the time it took them to dismount and tie their animals, they were under close scrutiny of the guard and several other men. They also noted the cigar-smoker in shirtsleeves framed in a cabin doorway.

"He Mister Chilson?" asked Larry.

"Who's askin'?" one of the men demanded.

"I'm Lawrence," offered Larry. "My partner here is Woodville. We rode here from the county seat to talk with Mister Chilson, if he can spare us a little time."

"I'll talk with 'em, Griff," called Chilson.

Side by side, the tall men walked from the picket-line to where Chilson stood. Confronted by them, he frowned curiously.

"You wanted to talk to me?"

"Well, yeah, but maybe you don't want to hear nothin' from me," Larry said contritely, moving forward to stand beside him. "You see — uh — it was me got shot at by Mister Javert and I'm powerful sorry about that. I still don't savvy how it happened and . . . "

"Well . . . " shrugged Chilson.

"I mean I sure didn't want to kill him," muttered Larry. "Had to defend myself, you know?"

"Tragic business," said Chilson. "But you had no choice."

"I'm mighty thankful you feel that way about it," said Larry. And then, so swiftly that Chilson could only gape, he emptied his holster. "I'll be extra thankful if you'll freeze, you murderin' sonofabitch."

Stretch, hearing the other men stirring, whirled and called a warning.

"No rash moves! Use your eyes! My partner's coverin' your boss!"

"Anybody tries anything, he goes first," growled Larry. With his cocked .45 rammed against Chilson's ribs, he delivered his ultimatum. "Call 'em out — all of 'em. I want to see your whole lousy crew out of those tunnels and grabbin' sky."

"You're crazy!" gasped Chilson.

"Not crazy, just lucky," countered Larry. "Lucky enough to hear Javert name Mosser's killer before he died — and lucky enough to find the message Mosser left for the sheriff."

"Wynant's in jail," Stretch drawled over his shoulder. "They never did get to try Doc Beaumont, but they'll sure as hell try Wynant."

"And you," scowled Larry.

At that, Chilson went berserk and yelled to his men.

"Every man for himself! Shoot your way out!"

Three more men, all brandishing guns, promptly charged out of a tunnel. Just as promptly, Stretch exhibited his lightning double draw, but without deterring the opposition. He crouched as they opened fire, chose targets and cut loose, while Dorgan and his deputies bounded into view with shotguns at the ready.

"Drop the guns!" bellowed Dorgan.

"In the name of the law!" yelled Tragg.

Chilson made to grapple with Larry, but not fast enough. The barrel of the Colt slammed to his temple and put him down like a poleaxed steer. Then the over-stimulated Ben discharged a barrel of his shotgun and Larry sidestepped with his six-gun booming. His target, a hard case fanning wild shots at the lawmen, reeled and collapsed with his chest bloody. Two more gun-toters appeared in the entrance to another shaft, both leveling rifles, and Stretch's matched 45's roared again. Wounded, one of the riflemen dropped his weapon and raised his hands. The other had fired only once before taking a bullet dead-centre.

The survivors, in shock and menaced by three Colts and as many shotguns, decided to heed Dorgan's demand.

"It's over! You don't stand a snowflake's chance in hell!"

It *was* over, and very quickly, and young Ben could barely believe it. Tragg had to repeat his command to rouse him to action.

"I said collect guns, kid. And start saddlin' horses."

Dorgan sidled to where the unscathed Texans stood and, while they reloaded their Colts, bent to stare at the senseless Chilson.

"Out cold — I mean *really* out," he muttered. "What'd you hit him with?"

"Just my hogleg," shrugged Larry. "Happened to be holdin' it on him. Seemed the right idea at the time."

"I didn't want any bloodshed,"

scowled Dorgan.

"Us neither," grunted Stretch. "But that's how it goes, Jerry. Even with Larry's gun proddin' him, the boss-thief hollered at 'em to shoot."

"Damn fools followed his orders," drawled Larry. He holstered his gun, fished out his making and began rolling a smoke. "Got some tidyin' up now, Jerry. Dead hombres to be wrapped and tied down, wounded hombres to be taken to town for doctorin'. Stretch and me, we'll be glad to help."

"Gee, thanks," sneered Dorgan.

"What're friends for?" grinned Stretch.

"I'd be obliged," sighed Dorgan, "if one of you'd head down to the bend and fetch our horses."

"On my way," said Stretch.

To the rear of the shafts, also in the cabins, Larry and the sheriff found cached gold, a lot of it.

"Some they maybe mined, most they hijacked," guessed Dorgan. "Hell, what a chore I'm gonna have. It'll take *weeks* for every loser to claim and collect his share. There'll be smart-alecks that never even *saw* a raider comin' by to claim this stuff."

"You'll have to leave a man in charge here," opined Larry.

"Right, and I already decided," nodded Dorgan. "Sam's the man. In this high country, there's no joker could bluff *him*." He checked his watch. "If we move slick enough, we could make town by sundown."

In less than a half-hour, they were ready to begin the journey to Cluff City. To the younger deputy fell the chore of leading the death-horses by a tie-rope, the Texans having volunteered to help guard the live prisoners. Tragg didn't protest the assignment wished on him by his boss.

"I should fret?" he grinned. "Got my hogleg, three scatterguns, plenty ammunition . . . "

"And you'll sure eat regular, Sam," remarked Ben. "A lot of provisions here and a stove and all."

"There'll be honest losers — like

Scudder and Pitney — and there'll be scavengers," Dorgan warned Tragg. "The shootin' must've been heard, so somebody's bound to get curious after we're gone."

"I can handle the curious ones," shrugged Tragg. "They'll find me ready and willin' to answer as many questions as they want to ask. From behind a cocked gun."

"I'll depute some volunteers and relieve you soon as I can," promised Dorgan.

"Better fetch an assayer too," said Tragg. "He could be mighty useful."

Later that afternoon, out of the foothills and pushing on toward the county seat, the victors of the Grand Venture shootout got to talking again. Larry made his and his partner's position clear by congratulating Dorgan.

"Congratulations — for what?" frowned Dorgan.

"What d'you mean — for what?" challenged Larry.

"You don't savvy plain English,

Texas-style?" drawled Stretch. "We're congratulatin' you for nailin' the skunk that backshot Mosser and the whole Grand Venture gang too."

"Does this mean what I think it means?" growled Dorgan.

"Well, that jasper, him that runs the newspaper, he's just bound to ask questions," suggested Larry.

"Ralph Gibb?"

"Yeah, him. You know how we are, Jerry. We don't need our names in no newspaper, but it's different for you. Be mighty encouragin' for the tax-payers of Gomez County, readin' of how their sheriff and his deputies wiped out these lousy gold-thieves, rounded up the whole gang."

"Forget it, Valentine. I don't intend lyin' to Gibb or anybody else. Besides, he's no fool. If he didn't see us ride out together, he'll certainly see us bring this bunch in. So you and Emerson get your share of glory again, like it or not."

"Glory," winced Stretch.

"A reputation," grouched Larry.

"Who needs it?" complained Stretch.

"Town'll settle down again now," Dorgan predicted. "Still wild. Still more chores than me and my deputies can handle. But better than it was. At least everybody'll realize no man gets away with murder in my bailiwick."

"And the Sierra Rojo is dangerous territory for gold-hijackers," remarked Stretch.

"And you tearaways'll get restless, now that you've cleared your dude buddy," Dorgan said pointedly. "Listen I got to say it. I appreciate everything you did, but I'll breathe some easier when you leave. No offense, but *when're* you leavin'?"

"Answer me somethin' first," frowned Larry. "How's it gonna be for the Queels from here on? You got any ideas?"

"They're here to stay," Ben gleefully assured them.

"Yeah, here to stay," nodded Dorgan. "All right, Valentine, you asked and I'm tellin' you. They'll be fine. With Little Nick courtin' Miss Prudence . . . "

"Nick Bolt's courting Ruth!" Ben said sharply. "*I'm* courting Prue!"

"No need to yell at me, boy," chided Dorgan. "As I was sayin', with Little Nick courtin' Miss Ruth, the whole Bolt family, meaning Big Nick himself and all his hired hands, are gonna be mighty protective of the little lady and her folks. And, seein' as how Marcus is courtin' Miss Angeline . . . "

"He's courting Josie," corrected Ben. "Angie's the youngest. Nobody's courtin' her yet."

"All right, *down* boy!" sighed Dorgan. "Hell, they all look alike. How do I know who's who and who's the youngest or oldest? What I'm sayin', Valentine, is all the best people of this territory are gonna rally round the Queels. That means all the reformers that want to improve Cluff City, like Big Nick, the deacon, the mayor and his alderman friends — all the folks that matter. So that answers your question.

The Queels'll be fine. They got it made while ever Mrs Queel cooks such elegant grub and her girls sing so purty."

"Sounds like they don't need us no more, runt," Stretch said wistfully.

"I reckon not," shrugged Larry.

"So answer *my* question," begged Dorgan.

"Soon, Jerry," said Larry. "We'll be leavin' real soon."

Regaining consciousness with a raging headache, finding himself in a cell-bunk in the county jail, the once wily Chilson suffered a chain reaction, first fury, then frustration followed by panic. To Dorgan, he pleaded that Wynant had disobeyed his instructions. He had never directed Wynant to dispose of Mosser, nor had he planned raids on other claims in the Sierra Rojo. Those raids had been planned and led by Javert without his knowledge. Overhearing this outburst, Wynant lost control and demanded to be let into Chilson's cell long enough to strangle him. Recriminations were hurled back and forth while Dorgan and Ben listened intently and the obliging Theo Haskin took notes.

Not until sundown did Doc Beaumont seek out the men to whom he owed so much. After retrieving his property from the sheriff, he had taken time to reflect on the turnabout achieved by the Texans and grudgingly reached the conclusion his manners left something to be desired.

They were propping up the bar in a downtown saloon, partaking of pre-supper drinks, when the elegant gambler-medico joined them. He dropped money on the bar, ordered bourbon, eyed them sidelong and addressed them very formally.

"Being a gentleman, I am obliged to acknowledge my indebtedness, express my gratitude and offer an apology."

"Think nothin' of it," drawled Stretch.

"And, if it makes you feel any easier, it was just the breaks, mostly loco luck, that put us wise to how you were set up," offered Larry. "Plain truth is I ain't no hot shot detective. I just learned a thing or two when it counted for most."

"Thunderation," sighed Doc. "I *hate* to be beholden to you two."

"Don't feel bad about it," grinned Larry. "You've pulled us out of many a tight fix."

"I insist this is one I owe you," retorted Doc. He sampled his bourbon and grimaced. "A debt of honor."

"Forget it," urged Stretch.

"Would that I could," muttered Doc. "Dare I enquire, is it too much to hope for, that you intend leaving Cluff City?"

"Manana," grunted Larry. "We'll shake Marv Queel's hand, hug his womenfolk and just check out. Dorgan don't need us no more. Seems Chilson and Wynant shot off their mouths, so he's got 'em cold. County prosecutor's jumpin' for joy. You leavin' too, Doc?" He winked at Stretch. "We could travel together — three old buddies."

"An utterly distasteful thought," snorted Doc.

"Stayin' on, huh?" prodded Larry.

"High Card Hemingway arrives tomorrow, according to my friend Fogel," said Doc. "A sporting man of formidable skill. Renowned poker player from Kansas City — looking for action. I'll be here to oblige one I regard as a worthy adversary."

"Have fun," said Stretch.

"It should be stimulating," said Doc. "And profitable."

Around 9.45 of the following morning, he loitered on the sidewalk opposite the Queel Hotel. The sorrel and pinto, saddled with all gear secured, stood at the hitch-rail while their owners traded goodbyes with the Queels and their comely daughters, six Iowans of refined background who, as Sheriff Dorgan had predicted, were making their genteel mark on a town desperately in need of improvement.

The tall men then descended to their horses, slipped their reins, got mounted and started south along Main. Sighting Doc Beaumont, they waved cheerily and called to him.

"Hasta la vista."

"We'll be seein' you. Bound to run into you again."

Watching them ride out, Doc winced resentfully.

"That's the hell of it," he reflected. "That's *my* hex. We undoubtedly *will* meet again."

THE END

TOP HAND
Wade Everett

The Broken T was big. But no ranch is big enough to let a man hide from himself.

GUN WOLVES OF LOBO BASIN
Lee Floren

The Feud was a blood debt. When Smoke Talbot found the outlaws who gunned down his folks he aimed to nail their hide to the barn door.

SHOTGUN SHARKEY
Marshall Grover

The westbound coach carrying the indomitable Larry and Stretch headed for a shooting showdown.

FIGHTING RAMROD
Charles N. Heckelmann

Most men would have cut their losses, but Frazer counted the bullets in his guns and said he'd soak the range in blood before he'd give up another inch of what was his.

LONE GUN
Eric Allen

Smoke Blackbird had been away too long. The Lequires had seized the Blackbird farm, forcing the Indians and settlers off, and no one seemed willing to fight! He had to fight alone.

THE THIRD RIDER
Barry Cord

Mel Rawlins wasn't going to let anything stand in his way. His father was murdered, his two brothers gone. Now Mel rode for vengeance.

ARIZONA DRIFTERS
W. C. Tuttle

When drifting Dutton and Lonnie Steelman decide to become partners they find that they have a common enemy in the formidable Thurston brothers.

TOMBSTONE
Matt Braun

Wells Fargo paid Luke Starbuck to outgun the silver-thieving stagecoach gang at Tombstone. Before long Luke can see the only thing bearing fruit in this eldorado will be the gallows tree.

HIGH BORDER RIDERS
Lee Floren

Buckshot McKee and Tortilla Joe cut the trail of a border tough who was running Mexican beef into Texas. They stopped the smuggler in his tracks.

BRETT RANDALL, GAMBLER
E. B. Mann

Larry Day had the choice of running away from the law or of assuming a dead man's place. No matter what he decided he was bound to end up dead.

THE GUNSHARP
William R. Cox

The Eggerleys weren't very smart. They trained their sights on Will Carney and Arizona's biggest blood bath began.

THE DEPUTY OF SAN RIANO
Lawrence A. Keating and Al. P. Nelson

When a man fell dead from his horse, Ed Grant was spotted riding away from the scene. The deputy sheriff rode out after him and came up against everything from gunfire to dynamite.

FARGO: MASSACRE RIVER
John Benteen

The ambushers up ahead had now blocked the road. Fargo's convoy was a jumble, a perfect target for the insurgents' weapons!

SUNDANCE: DEATH IN THE LAVA
John Benteen

The Modoc's captured the wagon train and its cargo of gold. But now the halfbreed they called Sundance was going after it . . .

HARSH RECKONING
Phil Ketchum

Five years of keeping himself alive in a brutal prison had made Brand tough and careless about who he gunned down . . .

FARGO: PANAMA GOLD
John Benteen

With foreign money behind him, Buckner was going to destroy the Panama Canal before it could be completed. Fargo's job was to stop Buckner.

FARGO:
THE SHARPSHOOTERS
John Benteen

The Canfield clan, thirty strong were raising hell in Texas. Fargo was tough enough to hold his own against the whole clan.

PISTOL LAW
Paul Evan Lehman

Lance Jones came back to Mustang for just one thing — revenge! Revenge on the people who had him thrown in jail.

HELL RIDERS
Steve Mensing

Wade Walker's kid brother, Duane, was locked up in the Silver City jail facing a rope at dawn. Wade was a ruthless outlaw, but he was smart, and he had vowed to have his brother out of jail before morning!

DESERT OF THE DAMNED
Nelson Nye

The law was after him for the murder of a marshal — a murder he didn't commit. Breen was after him for revenge — and Breen wouldn't stop at anything . . . blackmail, a frameup . . . or murder.

DAY OF THE COMANCHEROS
Steven C. Lawrence

Their very name struck terror into men's hearts — the Comancheros, a savage army of cutthroats who swept across Texas, leaving behind a bloodstained trail of robbery and murder.

SUNDANCE: SILENT ENEMY
John Benteen

A lone crazed Cheyenne was on a personal war path. They needed to pit one man against one crazed Indian. That man was Sundance.

LASSITER
Jack Slade

Lassiter wasn't the kind of man to listen to reason. Cross him once and he'll hold a grudge for years to come — if he let you live that long.

LAST STAGE TO GOMORRAH
Barry Cord

Jeff Carter, tough ex-riverboat gambler, now had himself a horse ranch that kept him free from gunfights and card games. Until Sturvesant of Wells Fargo showed up.

McALLISTER
ON THE
COMANCHE CROSSING
Matt Chisholm

The Comanche, McAllister owes them a life — and the trail is soaked with the blood of the men who had tried to outrun them before.

QUICK-TRIGGER COUNTRY
Clem Colt

Turkey Red hooked up with Curly Bill Graham's outlaw crew. But wholesale murder was out of Turk's line, so when range war flared he bucked the whole border gang alone . . .

CAMPAIGNING
Jim Miller

Ambushed on the Santa Fe trail, Sean Callahan is saved by two Indian strangers. But there'll be more lead and arrows flying before the band join Kit Carson against the Comanches.

GUNSLINGER'S RANGE
Jackson Cole

Three escaped convicts are out for revenge. They won't rest until they put a bullet through the head of the dirty snake who locked them behind bars.

RUSTLER'S TRAIL
Lee Floren

Jim Carlin knew he would have to stand up and fight because he had staked his claim right in the middle of Big Ike Outland's best grass.

THE TRUTH ABOUT SNAKE RIDGE
Marshall Grover

The troubleshooters came to San Cristobal to help the needy. For Larry and Stretch the turmoil began with a brawl and then an ambush.

WOLF DOG RANGE
Lee Floren

Will Ardery would stop at nothing, unless something stopped him first — like a bullet from Pete Manly's gun.

DEVIL'S DINERO
Marshall Grover

Plagued by remorse, a rich old reprobate hired the Texas Trouble-shooters to deliver a fortune in greenbacks to each of his victims.

GUNS OF FURY
Ernest Haycox

Dane Starr, alias Dan Smith, wanted to close the door on his past and hang up his guns, but people wouldn't let him.